SHIFTERS ANONYMOUS

A BANBURY SHIFTER TALE

MJ MARSTENS

Cover: Kadee Brianna at Everly Yours Cover Designs
Formatting: A.J. Macey at Inked Imagination Author Services

CONTENTS

BLURB

Who says you can't be smart and loose-legged?

The University of Oxford—*that's who.*
Meaning Jezebel Harper has a problem because the gorgeous American really wants to keep her scholarship.
What's a sex addict to do?
Join Sexaholics Anonymous, obviously—except, Belle doesn't read the fine print.
S.A. means something completely different.
Belle shows up at *Shifters' Anonymous*, where four drool-worthy males and two stunning women all turn to stare at her...
And, instead of being a solution to all her problems, S.A. is where Belle's all begin.
Get ready for a new spin on 'lost in translation'.

WARNING

Warning: This is a reverse harem romcom (comedy) series with explicit language and scenes for readers 18+. This is book one of **Shifters Anonymous.**

DEDICATION

For anyone who has ever felt not good enough—STOP.

YOU. ARE. WORTHY.

Please, remember this when you look in the mirror.
Also, for anyone who's wanted to try something crazy—
sexually—Belle encourages trying new things.
Unless it involves porcupines and pizza cutters.
That sounds dangerous.
And kind of intriguing.
Shit. . . anyone else envisioning a dashing naked porcupine
with a strap-on serving piping hot pizza?
No?
Me, neither.
And since you're still reading, this is for Annie and Allison
—my personal AA (Alpha's Anonymous). Thanks for
helping me curb some of Belle's crazier tendencies (i.e.
mine) and keeping me in line—we'll save those for Baba
Yaga.

Chapter 1

Belle

On paper, I'm everything the University of Oxford is looking for. In person—*not so much*. I'm a five foot four mess of brightly colored ombré-dyed hair, even brighter make-up, wearing high heels with jean shorts that do more to reveal than conceal. Where everyone else is sporting their trendy tweed blazers and hand-knitted, expensive wool cardigans, I'm flashing a whole lot of top-boob in my low-cut tank tops. Needless to say, Belle Harper *on paper* is smart and classy as fuck.

But Belle Harper *in person?*

Well, I'm some kind of beautiful train wreck—*but, it's working for me, I swear.*

It's summer in Oxford and I'm on break before I start my second year of my master's program here at the university. I'm studying Classic Lit; in case you're wondering. Also, I've slept with almost every student and professor—male or female—in case you were wondering that, too. And, now, I'm *booooooooooored.* No new students will really come in for another few weeks, which leaves me with. . .

My own sloppy seconds.

Normally, I would be cool with this because I'm a closet whore. Redaction—I'm just a whore. You can't be a closet anything if everyone knows about it, right? But, they don't care and I sure as fuck don't as long as I'm getting that D. Or P. I'm not picky. I like both. Why settle for one when I could have it *all*?

If you're getting the impression that I'm a sex addict, well, you would be right. BUT, there are way worse things to be—like a drunk, a junkie, an American who understands no British slang. I'm the latter. Do you know how many idioms we use daily? *A butt ton.* There's a lovely example for you now. What the hell is a 'butt ton'? Well, it's a shit ton. . . and down the rabbit hole we go. This is all fine and dandy *if* you understand the idioms; if you don't, things like *this* happens:

Professor: I can't believe you've taken on such a big load —you must want to be cream crackered.

Me: I love big loads! Please, cream all over my cracker!

Translation—

Professor: I can't believe you've taken so many classes— you must want to be exhausted.

Me: I love buckets of cum! Please, jizz all over my pussy!

And this, ladies and gentlemen, is my life.

So, you see, being a sex addict is not nearly as damning or complicated. I rest my case. I bet you're thinking it's a good thing I'm not here for law school and I would agree. I'm actually here on scholarship—*how fancy is that?!* It sounds impressive until you get an eyeful of me. Chances are I'm winking at you—because, well, we've established I'm addicted to what the dick, vag, balls, tit did to me.

It's right about now that you realize I need some help

and, Jesus save me, *I agree.* I can't even do my own sloppy seconds anymore! I don't want to wait for the new term's fresh blood. In fact, I kind of want to stop wanting sex so badly. Do you know how difficult it is to focus on Shakespearian literature when you're trying to eye-fuck your professor to see if he'll get a hard-on *in class*?

Clearly, I need some intervention.

Something like Alcoholics Anonymous—*but for whores.*

Whores Anonymous!

Skanks R Us?

Something!

I pull out my phone and begin searching. Low and behold, there *is* a group for people like me: Sexaholics Anonymous, or SA. Further investigation shows me there are no meetings in this area. Ugh, get it together Oxford, you bunch of prudes—I need help! But, when I keep scrolling, there is an upcoming SA meeting in Banbury, a city only thirty minutes north of here. That could work; I could borrow my friend's lorry—that's slang for truck and *not* his girlfriend. Boy, was George ever pissed when I took Laurie for a ride. *In my defense, he said I could take her for a drive...*

Clicking onto the link, I realize the meeting is *tonight* at eight. It's currently five, which gives me enough time to eat dinner and get ready. I have to look nice—*in case I meet someone.* Not for sex, though. Definitely not for sex. I just want to look cute. And slutty. I can't help that I don't own anything respectable. Fuck—am I going to have to start wearing cardigans after I finish the twelve steps? Those sweater things look itchy as all hell. I suppose wearing a bra would help...

Now, I have to go lingerie shopping.

Interesting fact: *bras and panties aren't meant to be worn just for seduction and roleplay purposes.* Apparently, they are everyday dress items. Huh, learn something new every day, right? I quickly go get a bite to eat and, then, head back to my single-room apartment to change. What's the dress code for a SA meeting? I mean, we've already established I'm not working with much, but I might have a dress that doesn't reach my navel and show off my ass at the same time. *Maybe.* Good thing Oxford doesn't have a dress code.

I finally find *one* respectable shirt, but it's long-sleeved and *red*. Red isn't really my jam right now, not with my magenta-to-purple-to-blue hair, but I feel like Oxford has an image to live up to—one I don't embody. And, if I don't get my shit together fast, they might withdraw my scholarship. I can't say this for sure, my grades are beyond stellar; it's just a hunch. Actually, more like a whispered rumor I'm sleeping with all my teachers to get good grades. I *am* sleeping with them, but the grades are all me, baby.

Who says you can't be smart and loose-legged?

Don't answer that.

So, red top it is. And since I'm going to clash, I decide to paint my nails and lips blood red, too. Oh, and line my eyes in blue. Not exactly like Mimi from *The Drew Carry Show*—*but close.* Apparently, the make-up experts say blue-eyed women shouldn't wear bright blue around their eyes. A tasteful and conservative navy, if you must, but stick to earthy browns and purples to make those baby blues pop. I say, 'fuck it', and wear an electric teal that looks slightly radioactive in the tube—*considering how I just rimmed my lower eyes with it, I sure as fuck hope it's not.*

I finish my ensemble with a pair of tight black jeans, glossy reddish-pink heels, and some chunky costume jewelry. It sounds over the top and totally is—*but that's my style.* It's very 'in-your-face' and blatant. I don't have time to be coy; I just want what I want. But, Belle Harper is turning a new leaf. No more sex, sex, sex, sex for me.

Jizz can no longer be part of my food pyramid.

Sexaholics Anonymous, here I come; *time to make me a new woman.*

Chapter 2

Belle

No one is really comfortable letting an American woman dressed as a night walker borrow their vehicle, so I end up taking a train to Banbury. I get a lot of looks on my journey north. Some are speculative—*they're wrong, I'm not a hooker, I'll screw their brains out for free*—others, suggestive, and some downright *hungry*.

I might not be a class-act, but fuck if I don't have sex appeal. I've seriously questioned if I might be a succubus or some shit. When I asked my mom, she hung up on me; so, I'm still not entirely certain. For the most part, I ignore everyone on the train, although I do send a group of nuns a wink. Their scandalized gasps are almost as good as a stranger slipping a hand under your skirt.

Yes, *I went there.*

We've already established that I desperately need help—which I'm getting. *Soon*. Once the train stops, I follow my phone to the old Anglican church. I'm still not sure if it's fitting or blasphemous to hold a sexaholics meeting in the basement of Christ's home, but who am I to judge?

I pull open the front doors and make my way downstairs. A group of men and women around my age are already gathered there in a circle of chairs. I'm not exactly nervous, per se, but my stomach flutters at the sight of them. As long as it's not my pussy fluttering, I'm going to make it out of this meeting a changed woman.

I sit down in a vacant chair and politely smile at all the other sex fiends in the room—and, then, *freeze*. There are two women and four men and, clearly, they put the 'sex' in 'sex gods'. They're absolutely gorgeous! Oh no. . . was Sexaholics Anonymous not for curing your sex addiction, but *for indulging in it?!*

I can't tell if I'm disappointed or excited at the prospect because, let me tell you—these people are *hot*. Maybe the group is Succubuses Anonymous? I've finally found my tribe. *Thanks for nothing, mom.* I had to do all the work myself. Please, insert some of your own internal grumbling for her lack of help.

I discreetly check everyone out—I mean, *assess*—from under my eyelashes. The two women have very dark hair, but one is styled into an adorable pixie cut and the other's is long and straight down her back. The woman with short hair has warm brown eyes *and freckles*. Frickin' freckles, I say. That, coupled with her lip piercing, makes me want to kiss her face.

The other woman is not as cutesy, but she has a rack on her that simultaneously makes my mouth water *and* makes me jealous—like, I want to motorboat her and boob-punch them for their large, perky perfection. I avert my gaze from her glorious pale globes—because I'm a recovering sex addict and I don't stare at strangers' tits—to her face, which is more acceptable to stare at.

Her eyes are a deep blue that contrasts lovely with her

dark hair and fair skin. Her lips are full and pouty, making me wonder what her other ones are like. . .and there I go again. Whelp, this is my first day of SA, I'm bound to have some relapses. If they are just mental ones, I'm calling that a win. The gorgeous woman arches a brow when I keep gawking at her like a creeper. No wonder the world thinks Americans are all impolite twits.

Step it up, Belle!

Although, in my defense, I'm not exactly a stellar ambassador for the American people in general.

I quickly look away to check out—fuck, I *totally* meant assess—the guys in the room. There are four of them and they are *built*. One has pitch-black hair, but it seems to glint red under the fluorescent lights, but the guy next to him is definitely a red-head. Hello, Mr. Gingerbread Man. Moving along, there's a blond man and the last guy has brownish-gray hair, but he's certainly not *old*. He must dye it that way. It sounds strange, but it's working for him.

Hell, everything on these dudes is working for them. I can only imagine what their co—*nope!* Not even going there. I will not, for one second, envision what their dicks look like. Or feel like. Or taste like. I'm going to need a lot of help, aren't I? I also think I need to find another SA group—one that is less *tempting*. Or, maybe, I need a buddy! Someone saintly, like a monk. . .

Now, I'm imagining seducing a monk.

Fuck.

When is this meeting going to start?

I need the help *now*.

The man with the dark black hair with red undertones must read my mind because he clears his throat to get everyone's attention before addressing the room.

"I don't think anyone else is coming tonight. Welcome,

everyone. I see that we have one newcomer; so, let's all intro-
duce ourselves."

His voice is liquid sex I want to pour all over my body
and roll in—*oh, I'm the newcomer, aren't I*? I sit up straighter,
proving that I can think with my brain and *not* my vagina.
Plus, I need to get everyone's names if I'm going to get their
numbers later—for that buddy system! If you're chanting
'liar, liar, pants on fire', well, that's just childish.

"I'll start," the sex god who just spoke volunteers.

His accent sends a shiver down my back. It's the smooth,
refined British one that totally would make any woman take
off their panties at the sound of it—thank God I'm not
wearing any right now, or else I would be making a fool of
myself.

"I'm Jude and I'm a cockchafer."

"Hello, Jude," everyone says together—*except for me.*

I'm too confused to say much. See—this is where
knowing the lingo would really help. Is cockchafer a British
word for 'cock chaser'? Does this sex god only like dick?
Now, that's a seriously depressing thought. Mr. Ginger interrupts my musings.

"I'm Arthur and I'm a horny toad."

My mouth flaps open at his brutally honest words. This
man might be horny, but I wouldn't call him *a toad*, by any
means. The blond man goes next.

"I'm Theo and I'm a fucking slippery dick," he spits out
in obvious distaste.

Man, *and I thought that I was hard on myself about my
addiction. . .*

The man with the brownish-gray hair snorts.

"Whatever. I'm Jack, *the Ass.*"

Does that mean he's really into anal?

I should probably ask him—just for clarification's sake.

The cute girl with freckles chuckles.

"Well, at least you aren't a blue tit! The name's Sian, by the way," she adds on for my benefit.

I've never heard of a woman called 'Shawn'. Maybe her mother forgot to add the 'a' at the end?

The woman with the delicious rack rolls her eyes.

"And I'm a blue booby. I'm Elise."

Now, everyone looks at me expectantly, but I have no freaking clue what to say to any of this. Whatever I stumbled across has to be the most hardcore SA group on the face of the Earth! Instead of just admitting to their problems, it's like they're doing a British roast of themselves. I've never even been to an *American* one, but I've seen a couple on TV.

It's brutal—but, kind of refreshing.

Maybe this is *exactly* what I need.

Beaming a smile at everyone, I take my turn.

"Hello, everyone. I'm excited to be here and *finally* seek the help I need. I'm Jezebel," I announce, using my full name for once because, really, it's fitting as fuck. "And I'm a horny, slippery-dick-loving, mouse-clicking pussy."

Chapter 3

Jude
THE COCKCHAFER

I blink at the odd, but stunning, woman's confession.

Was she saying that she's a cat shifter?

Why would a cat shifter be *here*?

Maybe she was a sphynx cat or some shit. I can see that being a real downer—especially if this is her human form, but she doesn't appear particularly feline. Maybe she is a half-breed? It certainly would explain why I smell *human* on her.

I think about the rest of her ridiculous sentence. What the bloody hell was a horny mouse-clicker? Is it some strange and spined rodent? Or, is it like the titmouse and not like its name at all? FYI: titmice are a type of bird, just ask Sian. Does she ever get pissed off when someone doesn't know what a titmouse is, even though she's specifically a blue tit.

I get it, though.

How many people know what a cockchafer is?

I decide to ask this to the new girl—*Jezebel*. What a name. Fuck. What a body.

"I know this is your first meeting and everything, but do you know what a cockchafer is?" I ask as politely as I can because it really is unfair to do this to a new member.

I'm just curious—no one ever knows. Every other animal with cock in their name—peacock, cocker spaniel, cockatoo, even just cock—they get recognized. *Me?* I'm lower than a bug, forgive my pun.

"Erm, no, not really," she admits. "I'm terrible with my British slang. I thought it might mean—wait! Cockchafer. . . like to chafe?"

She rubs her hands together in excitement to mimic her words.

"I get it now—you *chafe cocks*! You bring dead boners back to life! You're like a cock doctor or something! Oh my god, thank you so much for your work! I didn't even know that was a thing, but you're my hero. I feel like chafing cocks would be a lot like being a masseuse. I just don't have the hand stamina. Don't get me wrong—I give a mean hand job; I just don't want to do it for hours. I use my mouth a lot with it, usually. So, it's more like a blow-slash-hand job. . . a bland job? No, that's a terrible blending of the two words. A how job? I've got nothing. Next meeting, I will," she swears.

I sit there, with my hands in the universal 'what-the-fuck-is-happening' gesture, looking at my fellow oddball shifters. Jack is laughing hysterically, not bothering to cover his humor. Theo looks torn between amusement and horror. Sian and Elise are staring at Jezebel like she is their new favorite pet, and Arthur looks completely gobsmacked —which is *exactly* how I feel, too.

"N-n-n-o," I finally manage to stammer through my perplexity. "I'm an insect."

Jezebel frowns severely at me, drawing my attention to her pouty red lips.

"Ok, I'm going to be honest. I think it's great that we're here to get the help we need, and the roasting is a little funny, but you are all *way* too hard on yourselves! Just because I'm a coward with a problem doesn't mean I'm not a good person. The same goes for everyone in this room––you are all perfect the way that you are!"

She nods her rainbow-colored head twice to punctuate her words; then, winces.

"Well, I mean, *you all* are perfect the way that you are. . . me, on the other hand, not so much," Jezebel confesses sadly.

"Bollocks!" Sian spits. "If we're good enough, then so are you, love."

The lovely newcomer perks up.

"Thank you. That makes me feel so much better. It's so nice to be in the company of others who are struggling with the same problem."

"If I can be so indelicate to ask, but what kind—"

"Am I? I don't take offense. I'm sort of a. . . mutt, you could say," Jezebel answers with a chuckle. "Into everything, I guess."

I gape at her in horror as her words sink in—*a mutt?!* No wonder she's an outcast! Half-breeds are considered an abomination—and, clearly, she is half-human—but her shifter side is mixed, too! Another taboo in our society. Shifters don't mix species. It's barely acceptable to procreate within the same genus. Shifters are proud creatures who are similar to ancient monarchs—they want to keep their bloodlines as pure as possible.

The others all stare at her with similar looks of pity and understanding. We started this group because we are the lowest of the low. Our animals are considered jokes within the shifter community—and that's excluding our names, which add to our outsider status.

"Wow. . . *a mutt*," Arthur mumbles. "And I thought being a horny toad was bad."

"No—it's just as bad," Jack brays. "We should have made this the SSA for the Shitty Shif—"

"We're *not* shitty," Jezebel cuts in. "We're. . . super! The first 'S' now stands for super!"

Sian and Elise clap while Theo chuckles.

"I like it—no one's ever called me 'super' before," he admits.

Jezebel's eyes twinkle as she slides him a wink.

"You look pretty super to me," she all but purrs and, for the first time, I see something feline in her.

Theo makes a choking sound and blushes. Water shifters are not particularly popular since most are rarely in their element to shift. Lager marine predators get more respect—but, again, they are of no use unless near water. *But slippery dicks?* They just get laughed at—because of their size *and* their name. I'm sure Theo isn't used to women hitting on him, especially other shifters. But, Jezebel did mention that she is a 'slippery dick lover'. . .

Maybe that's another reason she's an outcast?

"Th-th-thanks," Theo stammers.

Jezebel sends him a brilliant smile before frowning again.

"I think we need a buddy system," she announces.

"A buddy system?" Arthur wonders.

"Yes, especially me since I'm down in Oxford. We need

to pair up together to support one another. Have a 'call whenever for whatever' policy to ensure that we are doing ok and aren't going to *relapse*."

Relapse?

What the hell is this woman into?

But Sian and Elise seem completely on board. In fact, everyone is on board and exchanges numbers with Jezebel, who appears over the moon. My heart softens to see her glowing with happiness. I can't imagine that she has a lot of friends and I'm glad that she's finally found others who will accept her unequivocally.

"This was an *interesting* meeting, but I'm so glad that you joined us, Jezebel. Next meeting, barring we have no new members, I would like to start addressing how we can positively contribute to society and start earning the respect that we deserve," I proclaim.

"Oh!" Jezebel gasps in delight. "That's just perfect—exactly why I joined. I definitely need pointers on how to gain respect. Let's make it a potluck and meet an hour early. What does everyone say?"

"That sounds delightful," Arthur concurs and everyone else agrees.

"Wonderful! I'll bring something American for you all to try! I have everyone's number and you all have mine. Well, not *you*, Mr. Cockchafer," she adds with a sultry look in my direction that has my body humming in awareness, "but you can get it from Jack or someone else. Please, call me day or night if anyone needs *anything*. Until next week!"

She blows us all a kiss and practically skips away.

"What. . . what the fuck just happened?" I mumble out loud, making Sian giggle.

"I don't know, but I love her already," she attests.

"As long as her 'American' meal isn't burgers and fries," Jack jokes and I grin.

An absolutely gorgeous American half-breed shifter mutt. . .

Now, I've seen it all.

Chapter 4

Belle

I practically run from the basement before I shame myself and jump someone, *but who could blame me?* With all that muscle, soft skin, and raw sensuality, it's like my fellow SA members were *begging* me to get down and dirty with them.

I hoped for a little more from the meeting, but I understand that I kind of derailed everything as the newcomer. Everyone seems genuinely shocked about my sexual involvement in . . .well, *everything*. Apparently, they all only had individual vices. For that, I'm envious. It would be so much easier to ignore my addiction if I only craved large veiny dicks with a left curve, right? It would seriously narrow down my options.

But when you want to fuck anyone and everyone?

Well, it's like dropping a kid off in a candy store and telling them that they can only smell and look, but never touch and taste.

Basically—*impossible.*

I spend the rest of my return trying not to masturbate

openly on the train. You read that right—I totally got myself off before a bunch of strangers. I mean that's a turn-on in itself. Fuck. . . *is this my first relapse?* No, you can only have those *after* you've completed the program. Phew. Ok, I'm still on track.

But, no more clicking the mouse.

Wait—*is that even a rule?*

Is that even fair?!

I mean, alcoholics abstain from hard liquor, but they can have wine and shit, right?

I pull out my phone and search, but nothing helpful really comes up. On a real downer note, apparently, recovering alcoholics can't have *any* kind of booze. *Can you believe that?!* If I'm following that terrible directive, does that mean sex *with myself* is off-limits, too? Time to ask a fellow SA member.

Which is totally *not* a ploy to text one of them!

Who would most likely be helpful and down for a little sexting?

Oh, Jesus, is sexting banned, too?

I'm going to need a freaking list of what I can and cannot do.

The slippery dick probably knows. I bet he'll be happy to lend me a hand. Maybe some fingers. Maybe his whole fist. We'll see how I'm feeling after we talk.

BELLE: Hey, you super slipper dick 12, is clicking the mouse something I can still do?
THEO: . . .
BELLE: You know, can I pet my kitty?
THEO: It's your kitty, right? We encourage one another to accept our other forms. So, pet away, I guess?

BELLE: Thank fuck! Wanna send me a pic of *your* slippery dick, pretty please 12?
THEO: Sure... here you go.

I'm practically bouncing in my seat from excitement—both from knowing I can still finger-fuck myself to sleep *and* because Theo's going to show me his cock. I always love a good dick pic. I don't care how uncouth Oxford thinks I am, but Brett Favre can send me shots of his open fly *anytime*.

About five minutes later, Theo's pic finally comes through. What was he doing? Getting the right lighting?! I open it up and find... *a fish in a tub?* It's taken at the weirdest angle, like the phone is propped up against something and, for the life of me, I can't figure why the guy sent me *this*.

I think I could live in England my entire life and still never understand British humor.

BELLE: Very cute.
THEO: Thank you! The coloring you see down the side is rare.

I stare at my phone.
What a strange dude.
Why does that turn me on?
Because everything turns you on, my mind snarks.
Shut up, bitch-brain, I snark right back. *I'm getting help!*
Now, I wonder if I need help for talking to myself.
Eh, one problem at a time, right?
By the time I make it back to my apartment, it's nearly ten and I'm exhausted. Just as I'm about to pass out, Theo texts me again.

THEO: Since you asked me, can I see your kitty?

BELLE: *See it?* I'll let you do a helluva lot more to it, but here's a pic to tide you over.

I snap him an up-close and personal shot of my snatch and fall asleep with a grin on *both* my sets of lips.

The next week flies by—*thankfully*—and it's Thursday night again. Time for my second SA meeting. We're meeting at seven and I need to bring food, per my suggestion, but now I'm in a quandary. Where am I going to get 'American' food? You can't bring British McDonalds to a potluck, can you? Why the fuck are there so many arbitrary rules in the world?!

Finally, I decide on tacos. They're technically Mexican, not American, and I'm sure I'm getting that wrong, too, but who doesn't love a good taco? I know I do—*pun totally intended.* I spend the train ride north thinking of all the terrible sexual innuendos I can make about tacos.

1. You stuff them with meat and, then, top them with cream.
2. Eating them is messy and the meat juice runs down your chin.
3. You can add some lettuce, tomatoes, and onions —basically a *tossed salad* on top of your taco.

Makes me wonder when the last time was that some-body tossed my salad. *Too long,* I tell you, *too long.* I frown and look down at my black nails, no longer painted their sultry red—black seemed more *professional.* I really need to reign in my thoughts. I toss my tie-dyed hair over my shoulder in contemplation.

Tonight, I'm wearing a black dress and heels to match my nails, but I refuse to change my hair. A line in the sand needs to be drawn and that's where it's going—*Oxford can kiss my sexually active ass on that one*. I also tried to tone down my makeup. Instead of bright pops of color, I've left my lips neutral and glossy, and I've only added a small cat-eye with my black liner.

The train stops and I make my way to the church, my arms laden with delicious tacos. I'm glad that Banbury is small and relatively low on crime since I'm a girl on foot—in heels and with precious food that I refuse to drop if I have to run.

Rule number one—*never waste food*—which wars with my 'always wear a condom or swallow' rule.

I'm like Julia Robert's hooker in *Pretty Woman*—*always a safety girl*.

Chapter 5

Belle

When I arrive in the community room in the basement of the church, everyone greets me warmly. *I freaking love this group.* They aren't all hoity-toity like most people I have to deal with on a daily basis back at the university. Surprisingly, there are some people I just can't seduce—usually only older women—and they get remarkably pissy with me when I continue on my merry way with everyone else around me.

"You look *lush*, love," Sian says to me as I set down my food.

I turn and give her a hug, which she returns. Unintentionally—*mostly*—I rub myself against her and she chuckles.

"Definitely a cat shifter," she laughs.

"If that's British for alluding to my shaved cat, then I dig it."

"Shaved, you say?" Arthur, my favorite horny toad, asks.

"Yeah, it's sexier that way," I wink at him. "But, sometimes, I leave a patch of hair."

Arthur and Jude visibly blanch at my words. I expect someone who's only into chafing cocks to not enjoy vag, but Arthur's reaction surprises me. *Maybe he only digs 1980s' pussy?* Well, I can certainly let my thatched roof grow back over my clam cottage if that's what he's into.

"I brought tacos!" I announce, turning the subject.

From this point on—no more innuendos. . .

But, *it's so fucking hard.*

Also, that's what she said, bahahahaha.

Sorry, I swear that I'm twenty-nine and not twelve.

Would a twelve year old even get that joke?

"Tacos?" Jack says with his bushy brows raised.

I notice that they, too, are tinted gray. This guy is *dedicated.*

"Yeah, I love tacos," I say with an eyebrow waggle at Elise and Sian.

Shit—*was that an innuendo if I actually really do love tacos?*

Correcting my errant possible sexual thoughts is fricking exhausting.

"That's not very *American*," Jack observes, and I stick my tongue out at him.

"It's the best that I could do—did you want hamburgers from McDonalds?" I sneer, but Jack just laughs.

"That's what I was counting on you to bring, love," he counters, and I roll my eyes.

"Don't be an ungrateful ass—it's *tacos.* Who says no to a good taco? I sure as fuck don't."

Everyone laughs.

"What did you bring?" I demand to the gray and brown haired man.

"Toad in a hole—a perfectly British dish."

23

"Sounds delightful," I lie since I have no idea what Toad in a hole is. . . hopefully, *not* like it sounds.

"I brought haggis," Arthur the Horny Toad declares.

"Isn't that like sheep's balls?"

"Sheep's pluck, actually—the liver, heart, and lungs wrapped in their stomach casing," Arthur corrects.

I grimace.

"Balls would have been a better choice—we could have dipped them in BBQ or some shit, but good job with choosing a non-suggestive food," I commend.

The others tell me of their food choices, and I struggle to keep my face straight. What kind of potluck is this? More like a potfuck—actually, that just sounds like a leprechaun orgy waiting to happen. . .and, now, I'm thinking of mythical creatures boning. That's just great. Although, for argument's sake, I feel like the 'Chauns are probably packing some serious gold coinage, if you know what I mean.

I imagine that they're well-hung for anyone not under-standing me.

"What are you thinking about? You have the funniest look on your face," Jude wonders.

"Elf sex," I blurt out and Jude's face goes blank.

Then, he—*and everyone else*—busts up laughing.

"I never know what you're going to say. I can't tell if that's an 'American thing' or a 'Jezebel thing'."

"Definitely a 'Jezebel thing'. Please, please, *please* don't judge my fellow Americans based off your perceptions of me," I lament.

"Why?' Theo asks in genuine confusion. "You're sexy, funny, nice—what's not to like?"

My smile splits my face at his words. I'm used to compli-ments—but that doesn't mean I still don't enjoy hearing them. Also, I totally forgive him for not sending me a real dick pic like I wanted, but Theo is a better friend for it. He clearly doesn't want me straying down a very dangerous and *cock*-eyed path.

Bad pun?

I've got more, don't worry.

We all chat amicably as we eat. I sample a little of everything and find—to my delighted astonishment—I like it all. I haven't really branched out much culturally since moving to England. I used to think we were similar. Hell—I used to think we spoke the same language, but I was w-r-o-n-g. Coming to Oxford was like entering a whole new world.

But, even for our differences, I feel at home with these four men and two women. Maybe it's our sexual deviancies and struggles that bring us together but, for the first time since moving here, I actually don't consider myself a pariah. I mutter this around a mouthful of bread pudding and the others look at me with soft eyes. My heart kind of melts like butter at their understanding gazes and I realize that they've been shunned, too.

For once, I don't lament my horny neediness—*because it brought me to some of the best people I've met yet.*

Chapter 6

Arthur
THE HORNY TOAD

I try not to stare at the captivating new shifter. We still don't know what she's a combination of entirely. Is it just two animals or more? Jude is certain that she's half-human, too, as if being mixed weren't enough. In all my years, I've never heard of something so strange. It's like an angel and demon having a child. I'm sure Jezebel would call it a 'demgel' or 'angmon'.

I smile as I watch her tuck into my mum's haggis. She's certainly a quirky one, but she seems to have the purest heart of gold. Throughout our meal, she asks us all where we live, what we do for a living, what our favorite hobbies are. . . she never even once mentions anything about our shifters. It's refreshing not to have to think or worry about my horny toad—*I can just be Arthur*.

I learn that she's studying modern literature at Oxford. I can't help the shocked expression that crosses my face at her words, but Jezebel doesn't take any offense. She explains how she even has their top scholarship to study, but she worries about how her image might tarnish that—that's why she's so excited for tonight's meeting.

I shoot Jude a confused look.

Did Oxford specifically have a program for shifters?

Our kind mingles with humans—but that didn't mean that they *know* about us. It's a strict rule in the shifter community that no human can know about our existence because of their penchant for being 'scientific assholes', as Jack calls them. Basically, if humans were aware of our existence, they would use the knowledge to exploit our differences, study us, and—*eventually*—run us extinct.

Shifters don't procreate like humans, the lucky bastards. Our mating process is a little more animalistic and follows specific periods for rutting and when our females go into heat. Some shifters lay eggs and produce more offspring that way but, generally, every animal is bound by some bestial rule.

For example, insect shifters might lay copious eggs, but only every so many years and only so many will survive. Mammal shifters generally tend to have only one living child in their entire lives. Aquatic and aviary shifters have to be in water or nesting—not something exactly conducive in the modern world—and so their numbers are low, too.

Jude shrugs at me and I read his body language perfectly —shifters are *everywhere*, how should he know? Shifters at Oxford, sounds like something pretentious and douchey that a Tertiary would do. I'm not trying to sound bitter, but I've lived my whole life being inferior—a *Primary*, or the lowest rung of shifter. Tertiaries are the apex shifters—think lions, tigers, wolves, and bears.

A horny toad really isn't that impressive in comparison.

Why couldn't I have been born a poison dart frog at the very least?

I pause my internal moping to tune into the meeting that Jude is now starting. Since no one is new, we skip the formalities and dive right into tonight's purpose: *how to become respected by Tertiaries.* Jezebel pulls out a notebook and a pen, and I think she is the cutest thing ever. She certainly takes our meetings seriously and who can blame her? She's considered a Secondary because of her cat blood, but I assume the other animal mixed-in is a Primary. Oh, *and* she's part *human.*

Even if one-third of her was *Tertiary* cat shifter, it still wouldn't negate the mutt-human mix.

"Tertiaries. . ." she sounds out slowly, writing down the word. "I'm assuming that's the higher ups?"

Jude exchanges a look with all of us.

I'm beginning to think that Jezebel really has no knowledge of our world.

"Jezebel," Jude starts.

"Actually, I usually go by Belle," she corrects.

"Belle is pretty," Jude compliments. "I assume you know that your. . .*other side* is from one of your parents, right?"

Belle stops writing and tips her head in bewilderment.

"What? No, I don't think that's right," she denies.

"It is," Jude insists. "You definitely are the way you are from either your mum or your dad."

"Are you sure? Is there, like, medical proof of this?"

"We're sure," Theo confirms. "All of us are proof."

Belle's eyes widen.

"Every one of your moms or dads is. . . *you know*?!"

"Well, both of our parents, actually."

"Both of them?!" Belle screeches. "How am I the only one into everything, then?"

Jack rubs his neck before answering.

"Because all our parents are the same—whatever we are, they are."

Belle sits back at this revelation. She looks like someone coshed her over the head with a hammer, the poor mite.

"So. . . my parents must be different, then?"

"Yes," Elise agrees. "They clearly are not the same type of animal."

"Like a 'whole other beast' thing, huh? I swear these idioms are going to be the death of me. Okay. Sorry—it's just so much to wrap my head around. Plus. . . I really don't want to think of my parents that way," she says with a disgusted face.

"How?" I ask.

I never realized how two people could speak the same language but not make any sense, and that's Belle in a nutshell—*she makes almost zero sense.*

"I don't want to imagine my parents mixing Ps and Vs!" she blurts. "Ew!"

"*Mixing Ps and Vs*" Sian wonders.

The rest of us shrug at her. The American shifter is a bit of a mystery. I'm going to need an American-English dictionary if I'm ever to understand her.

"Maybe you should ask them?" Jack suggests, but Jude and Belle shake their heads.

"No way! I'm not talking to my parents about that!" she protests vehemently.

"Besides," Jude inserts, "we can't assume anything. Both might be mixes or only one might be. It could cause chaos."

"Good point," Jack sighs. "Well, I'm sorry that this is such a revelation to you. I can't imagine having to learn about our kind on your own."

Belle lifts a shoulder delicately.

"I'm just glad that I've found you all. It helps to have others like me seeking help."

"Still—it's got to be a shock," I insist. I lean forward and lightly touch her hand. "Remember the buddy system you mentioned? We're all here for you—day and night. If you need *anything*, call me or someone else immediately."

Everyone nods emphatically in agreement and Belle's eyes begin to mist.

"Thank you," she says in a grateful and strained voice.

My heart bleeds for the sweet lass. I can't imagine having to learn and deal with all this on her own, but at least she's not alone anymore. This horny toad is sticking by her side forever.

Together, all of us are shitty shifters uniting to become super.

Chapter 7

Belle

My parents are closet sex freaks.

Wow.

That's...

Disturbing as fuck.

Honestly, I'm having a hard time imaging it. I mean, my dad wears a belt buckle and tucks in his shirt. His pants are always pressed, and my mom doesn't wear anything lower cut than under her chin—she owns a butt ton of turtle-necks. In fact, my clothing is the bane of their existence. If my parents could afford to come over the Big Pond for 'parent's day', Oxford would freaking adore them.

People have actually asked my parents if they adopted me.

Rude.

So, to learn that at least one of them is dirtier than a dollar bill left on a toilet seat is unsettling. I wonder which parent it is and quickly shut that thought down—thoughts bring visuals. And visuals of *that* bring nightmares and years of therapy that no psychologist has a hope of curing.

Although, if I am hazarding a guess, I would say it's my mother. I see her sliding side-glances at my dad all the time. I thought that they were silent reprimands, but now I'm wondering if they were invitations for, you know, *fucking*. A shudder racks my body at this—that's a lot of fucking invitations, *literally*.

Arthur looks at me with concern.

"Are you alright, lass? Is it too chilly in here?" he wonders.

"Maybe if she didn't shave her kitty-cat," I hear Jude mumble, and this makes me giggle.

Do they honestly think I'm cold because my hot dog hole is hairless?

"I'm fine. . . just thinking. I apologize, Mr. Chafer of Cocks—please, continue. You were saying something about Tertiaries, I think?"

"Yes, but it seems that I will need to explain—"

Jack cuts him off.

"No, thank you, Professor Too Detailed. We'll be here all flipping night and Belle doesn't have that much paper in her notebook. I'll explain it," the ashy-haired man insists. "So, you've got the Tertiary bastards, the Secondary cunts, and the Pri—"

"Jack!" Elise interrupts sharply.

"What? I'm only telling her like it is," he whines.

"I'll take it from here," Elise says regally.

"God, you're such a *boob*," Jack teases.

"But she's my favorite boob," Sian counters.

"And you're my favorite tit," Elise adds.

"Awww," I coo, laughing, "you're *breast* friends!"

Everyone chuckles at my terrible pun and some of my anxiety wanes.

"As the jackass was saying," Elise continues, "there are

three levels—Tertiaries, Secondaries, and Primaries. Tertiaries are your apex hunters and Primaries are your. . .slugs."

"Think of it this way," Jude interjects, "Tertiaries are your upper-class and Primaries are your lower-class. Secondaries, then, would be the middle-class."

I nod in understanding.

"So, we're Primaries working to be Tertiaries?"

"Oh, no, love. It doesn't work that way," Sian says softly. "We can never be Tertiaries."

Jack snorts.

"Who wants to be one of those cheeky toffs, anyway?" he demands as Theo scoffs.

"Really? You wouldn't jump at the chance of being one of them?"

Jack just shrugs at my slippery dick—I mean, at *the* slippery dick.

"We're just working towards gaining respect from the Tertiaries," Jude clarifies. "We can never be anything other than what we already are."

"Then, what's the point of this?!" I growl in frustration. "Why am I trying to be a better person if I can never change myself?"

"Hey now," Arthur chides, "remember how you felt when we put ourselves down? Don't you do it, either. What Jude is trying to say is that we will never be "upper-class", but we don't have to live by our "lower-class" labeling. First, we have to respect ourselves and the positive contributions we do bring to our community before we can expect anyone else to see us in the same way. So, instead of focusing on the negatives, what are some positives? How has being the way you are impacted your life for the better?"

I nibble my lip pensively.[1]

How has being a sex addict been for the better?

"Well, I guess one positive thing is I've made other people happy—playing with my pussy will do that," I joke.

"See?" Arthur beams. "You've brought joy to others by, er, letting them pet you?"

"Pet me, stroke me, fondle me," I elaborate, trying desperately *not* to think about anyone doing those things.

I suppose this is one of the steps: *talking about sex without getting all hot and bothered.*

I'm totally not either of those things right now. I'm more. . . libidinous. There are fifty shades of *horny* and I'm well beyond 'hot and bothered', but can I be blamed? We're talking about people touching my squish mitten, after all.

"Well, that's nice you're so comfortable with that side of you," Jude compliments.

Theo squints at me like he is trying to read my mind—he should be thankful that he can't.

That shit is *graphic*.

"Like. . .you let nippers pet you?"

"Sure, nippers, biters, lickers—I'm not picky."

Jack chuckles.

"Blimey, you're a bit of a nutter, love. Can't say I've let any nippers stroke my mane. There was a chap once who tried to ride me when I snuck out once and changed. The plonker was so trollied he didn't even blink when I started talking!"

Everyone laughs uproariously while I try to translate mentally. Did Jack just say someone tried to fuck him when he was younger—I assume, because he snuck out—and didn't care if he talked during said fucking?

"Was this in public?" I gasp.

"Right in front of the shop," he chortles. "Luckily, it was late, and no one was around since it's illegal to expose ourselves."

W-o-w.

Is it wrong that I'm kind of in love with Jack right now?

I mean, I already was kind of in love with all of them for being too sexy for their clothes.

But anal with a stranger in public—*that takes my admiration to a whole new level.*

Chapter 8

Belle

Envisioning Jack getting ass-plowed by some stranger in the town square does wonders for taking my mind off my parents—who potentially might have done the same thing.

Who knows how far gone *their* addiction is...

And, changing the subject.

"Okay, so we've established that there's some positive with the bad, but how do we get the "High and Mighty" to treat us better? Does it require not wearing fishnets and garters to day functions?" I whine.

I really don't want to give up my come-hither ensembles, but it makes sense that the first step to gaining respect is to look presentable. I just don't understand why a whole lot of tit showing can't be presentable. They're just boobs!

And I want to see them all.

Jude surprises me by saying that he doesn't think it matters what I wear.

"The only way we can gain their respect is by demonstrating that we are useful in society—that we have something positive to add, like Arthur pointed out, no matter how minimal."

"Really?" Jack derides.

"Really," Jude retorts sternly. "I want everyone to do what Belle did—find something positive and useful about our other self that contributes to our community. Spend the next week doing this one thing and, at our next meeting, we'll discuss how it impacted us."

Jack glares at him incredulously.

"I'm not fucking letting anyone ride me—and what are you going to do? Pollinate people's gardens?"

I guess that Jack is over being the receiver. No more taking it up the ass—this anal sex fiend apparently only wants to give it. I'm okay with that. I wonder if he needs volunteers…

"I love your euphemisms," I say, instead, applauding myself silently for not offering my behind as target practice for Jack's dick. "I've let a lot of people pollinate my garden, if you know what I mean, haha."

No one laughs.

Huh, tough crowd.

"Erm, so anyway," I cough to cover my embarrassment, "I don't understand how letting people pet my pussy is going to help with my problem."

"Because—the first step is accepting ourselves and our other sides. Embrace it completely!" Jude enthuses.

"Well, I swear that I already have and that's what brought me here, but ok. Sure. I'll play 'stroke my south mouth' longer than Lionel Richie—all night looooong," I sing in a terrible parody of the actual song.

"South Mouth?" Theo wonders.

"Another name for pussy," I clarify.

Sheesh.

I need to look up British words for *vag* asap.

"You named your. . . cat?" Jude chokes.

"You didn't name your cock?" I counter.

"Um, can't say that I have."

"Well, that seems like step one to accepting and loving yourself."

"And yours is South Mouth?" Sian wonders.

"No—it's Loosey."

"Lucy is a lovely name," Elise compliments and I blow her a kiss of thanks.

"But what name should I choose?" Jude ponders seriously.

I shrug.

"I don't know—I've never seen your cock."

"Cockchafer," he corrects in a strangled voice, making Arthur blush and Jack laugh uproariously.

"Careful, love, or else Jude's going to think you want a look at his parsnip."

I roll my eyes.

Only the British would use a bulbous root plant as an innu-endo for dick.

"If you want my input, I'm going to have to see you naked."

"Ooooo, you can name my tit if I can get starkers!" Sian sings.

"I'll totally name your tit. . .and your boob!" I grin at Elise, my mouth watering at the thought of seeing her rack.

"This isn't a bloody orgy!" Jude bursts out, making me pout.

"Spoilsport," I mutter. "Well, are you going to show me or not?"

"I will," Jack volunteers. "I'll let you name my ass."

He stands up with this announcement, and I can't help

but lean around and check out his denim-clad butt—*I'm not drooling, you are.*

"Are you late for something?" I drawl.

"Er. . . no, I don't think so. Why?" Jack asks in confusion.

"Because your ass has *fine* written all. . .hmm. . . I don't think that's how it goes—my pick-up lines need work. Usually, I just ask if you're DTF, ya know?"

Jack just shakes his head and chuckles.

"No, Belle, I don't know. Come on," he directs.

"Where are we going?"

"I'm going to show you my ass, but only to you."

"Booooo!" Sian and Elise jeer, making me giggle.

"I'll tell you all about it," I promise them with a wink as I scurry to catch up with Jack.

We leave the basement to the first floor, but Jack keeps climbing the stairs until we're all the way to the top. In front of us is a closet; to the left is the choir loft and to the right is the bell tower.

"I'll, uh, go undress in there," he says, hitching a thumb toward the choir loft.

"What?!" I exclaim. "Why?"

Jack squints at me in confusion.

"I'll ruin my clothes if I don't take them off first. . ." he trails off, giving me a *look*.

"Oh—I see! Here, let me take them off for you so you don't tear them," I offer with a wink.

Apparently, Jack is afraid he'll rip his clothes off and ravage me if he doesn't take them off in private. I mean, *he is showing me his ass*; so, does it really matter? But I don't want to make him uncomfortable—we are recovering addicts, after all.

"Ummmm," Jack practically stutters as I fall to my knees before him.

It's not sexual, *I swear*!

I'm just helping a friend out of his jeans so I can take a look at his ass.

Nope.

Nothing sexual about that at all.

I lick my lips in anticipation as I unbuckle his pants—*for naming his ass*!

Nothing else.

I promise that my intentions are only of the highest order. I also confess that I'm a sick liar. I do want to get better, but I want Jack and his fine ass.

Now.

Chapter 9

Jack
THE ASS

The breath wooshes from my lungs when Belle gracefully sinks to the floor. It takes everything inside of me to not pant.

She's just helping undress me...

Nothing wrong with that.

She just wants me to be comfortable with shifting, I remind myself.

I will my trouser snake to remain limp, but the fucker doesn't listen. All he knows is that the most gorgeous woman we've ever seen is on her knees before us —*undressing me.*

I swallow thickly, embarrassed that I can't keep my dick under control. I'm like a horny teenager who's about to have his first shag. A shudder rocks my body when she shimmies down my jeans.

The cool air hits my exposed skin and I shiver.

"It's brass monkeys," I mutter.

"Are you talking about your balls?" she wonders, and I choke on a laugh.

"No, love, it means that it's bloody cold," I explain.

She tilts her head as her eyes light up with understanding.

"Do you want me to warm you?"

"No," I manage in a strained voice. "My ass is hairy enough to keep me warm."

Her eyes enlarge at my words, and I wince.

"Sorry—I hope that wasn't rude, considering that you have a, ah, bare pussy."

I hope that I didn't offend her since sphynx cats don't have any fur and donkeys are shaggy motherfuckers, but she tips back her head and laughs instead.

"I forgot that you prefer your pussy hairy."

"No, that's not true!" I rush to reassure. "I'm sure yours is perfectly lovely."

Gads, I sound like a right git.

I don't know why I have the collywobbles. The truth is it's been yonks since I've been on the pull. And, even though I'm not here with Belle in that capacity, it still feels like there's something more going on between us. Everything she says sounds like a sexual invitation, but I know that it's not.

I clear my throat.

"Where were we?" I ask.

"I was helping you out of your jeans, and then, I was going to finish undressing you before I wrapped my mouth around your cock," Belle summarizes in a husky voice.

My jaw drops at her blatancy.

Apparently, I was wrong—*very wrong.*

Belle *does* want me sexually.

Before I can make a stuttering fool of myself, she puts

her words to action. She deftly hooks her thumbs in the waistband of my boxers and yanks them down to my knees.

My cock—who clearly understood the situation better than me—is already standing at attention and waiting.

True to her words, the lovely little Yank sets to work on polishing my knob. My knees nearly buckle under the intense pleasure of her mouth working me up and down, and I slap a hand on the wall next to me to brace myself.

Belle hums a bit as she sucks me off, and my eyes roll back inside my head. I admit that it's been yonks since I've done anything, er, sexually, but she blows every other experience out of the water.

Her hands soon join her lips in their work on my undercarriage, and I know I won't last much longer. Belle's tongue laps at the tip before she sucks it in, her teeth gently grazing me as she lowers herself to the base of my cock.

Blimey—Belle's a fucking goddess.

The talented woman pulls back and works her hands in tandem like she's trying to wring an orgasm out of me—and, boy, does she. Out of nowhere, it comes barreling down my spine, bursting forth like an explosion of ecstasy.

The wall barely holds me up while I ride it out.

When Belle's cleaned my dick of all the last drops of cum, she slowly sinks back on her haunches and looks up at me with a satisfied smile on her face.

"Ready for round two?" she queries.

"No," I croak. "I wasn't prepared for round one."

But my cock says otherwise and has already sprung back to life.

"Why don't you bring your fine ass over here and fuck mine?"

My tongue twists itself in its hurry to agree with her plan, and then, becomes tied when she masterfully shimmies out her clothes. Her body is. . . *perfection*. Her straw-berry creams[1] are large and full with tips kissed by the rosiest nipples.

They're stiff because of how cold it is and seem to weep for me to warm them up as Belle warmed me.

It takes all I have not to move—but I'm determined to visually savor the goddess in front of me before I pounce on her like a starving man.

I force myself to look past her impressive baps[2], down the smooth, flat perfection of her stomach, and down her endlessly long legs—they glow with the same golden hue as the rest of her skin.

Finally, I allow myself to gaze at the most private part of her body. The apex of her legs is bare—just as she joked—but with her legs together, they hide her pink folds.

Belle must read something on my face—my disappointment, perhaps—because she shifts to widen her legs so that I can see between them. I inhale sharply at the scent of her.

It's pungent, heady, and sweet.

Her sex calls to me like *I'm* a cat in heat—not to mention that the sight alone nearly undoes me—I can see her wetness, even in the dark, and I've never wanted anything as much I want to be buried deep inside of her.

The brilliant woman must read my mind because, before I can blink, she races toward me in a bounding leap and—literally—jumps me. Her long legs wrap around my torso, and she lowers herself nimbly onto my straining cock.

Bloody thing has damn near popped off me trying to lodge itself inside the lady.

I scramble to cup her arse and keep her anchored to me while she bobs up and down. Belle stares deep into my eyes, and a seductive smiles curls her lips. She licks them before lowering her mouth to mine.

My brain is short-circuiting between the feel of her tongue stroking mine versus the feel of her fanny squeezing my dick.

"Let me come quickly; then, you can fuck my ass," she whispers against my lips.

"Ahhhhhhhh," is all I can manage.

Belle starts slamming herself harder and faster, bouncing up and down on my cock until, suddenly, she tosses back her head and cries out. I can feel the rhythmic compression of her quim, and I blink in surprise at how quickly she peaked.

"Ok," she pants, pulling away from me.

I frown and scramble to pull her back, but stop when she starts dipping her fingers into her wetness. Entranced, I watch as she dances her digits from her pussy to her bum—back and forth, over and over.

Fuck me—the wee seductress is priming her arsehole with her own natural lubricant.

"Belle," I rasp in a hoarse voice.

"Yes, Jack?" she asks as she bends over and touches her toes.

My eyes bulge at the sight.

"I'm ready," she hints broadly.

Well, don't let it be said that I'm a total plonker[3].

I step behind her and run a hand down the satiny skin of her back. She shudders lightly at the sensation—she's so sensitive to my every touch, and I grin.

I can't wait to see how this cat shifter reacts to me in her arse.

Gently rubbing my bell end against Belle's cheeks, I relish the shiver that engulfs her body. Slowly, ever so slowly, I push into her—the tightness of her arse resists me at first, but then, she relaxes and I surge forward in a single stroke.

Together, we let out deep groans of pleasure.

I stand there for a beat, letting her adjust, but Belle rocks forward onto her toes and back to her heels to signal that she's ready. Gripping her hips hard, I piston in and out of her.

"Faster!" she moans, and I almost slip.

I don't know if I can go any faster, but I'm bloody well going to try. Whatever this American goddess wants, I will gladly give it to her—*and, apparently, she wants me.*

The pace I set is grueling. Sweat is pouring off of me and splashing onto Belle's back. Hopefully, this isn't a turn off—donkeys are hard-working, but perspire something terribly.

In truth, I doubt Belle even notices.

She's deep in the throes of passion, and I take a moment to admire everything about her, once more. I love her body, but I adore her abandon even more—she holds *nothing* back.

"I'm almost there again," she gasps, and I realize that she's been finger-fucking herself the entire time I pummeled her arse.

The sight and thought undoes me.

Without warning, I come again.

I try to hold back, but can't. Thankfully, Belle doesn't seem to mind—in fact, I think it's what sets off her orgasm. She lets out a sweet mewling cry that makes my knackers[4] pulse as she comes. We collapse in a heap on the floor, our harsh breathing the only sound.

I don't even raise an eyebrow when Belle eventually says that she wants to see the bell tower—I'm getting used to her quirky ways. She saunters through the door, naked, and up the stairs. Chuckling at her free spirit, I go to put on my jeans when I realize that I never showed her my ass.

I'm about to shift when I hear a muffled cry and the

sound of someone collapsing. Quickly, I dash up the stairs to find Belle passed out. I scoop her up in my arms and race down to the basement, praying that she's all right. I practically leap into the room where the others are waiting.

"What took you so—" Jude starts and, then, he stops when he sees Belle in my arms.

It dawns on me that she's still naked and I groan.

There's nothing like admitting you were going to show off your animal side and end up screwing instead.

Chapter 10
Belle

*D*o you ever wake up tangled in a mass of limbs and wonder, *what the fuck happened last night?*

No?

Oh, well, I do quite often; so, I'm not really surprised when I come to and that's exactly what's happened.

I'm not in a mass of tangled limbs, per se, just naked in someone's lap—Jack's, to be precise. My brain is all fuzzy, like I'm super hungover or maybe still drunk.

"What happened?" I ask Jack.

Ugh, I finally get to fuck one of these dreamy dudes and I can't remember it!

"You went to go have a look at the bell tower and, then, you went arse over tit, love."

"I did what to whose boob now?" I blurt.

Beside us, there's a chuckle, and I realize that Jude is crouching over me, tucking me in with the blanket.

"He means that you fell—well, fainted, actually. Are you ok?"

His words are gentle, and his eyes are tight with concern.

"Of course, I'm fine. Jack took me up there to show me his ass. . . we relapsed—I totally relapsed. I lured him down the path of temptation. I'm *so* sorry; this is al—"

I cut off, remembering *exactly* why I had passed out. I had gone up to the bell tower to get some fresh air and, of course, to taunt Jack some more as I walked away—so he could stare at the ass that he had just freshly plowed.

While staring out the window, enjoying the afterglow of sex that was sure to dwindle into guilt sooner than later, I saw two figures across the street move. I almost dismissed them when I thought, *why would they be lurking in the dark if they weren't out for a fuck-rendezvous?*

Like the creepy sex-addicted voyeur that I was—am—I decided to watch. The couple had an interesting dynamic. The man was a good foot and a half taller than the woman and *built*; whereas, she was a fragile, diminutive thing. The beefcake daddy had his hands around her throat, and I could hear her cries of pleasure from where I was.

Except, the longer that I watched, the more I realized that they weren't *cries of pleasure* but pleas to stop.

Usually, the safety word was—there was no safety word —but I swore that I could see the terror in her eyes from where I stood.

Just as I was about to turn around, to run and get help, the man's hand morphed into that of a *tiger paw* and slashed the woman across the throat. A silent scream welled up in mine as I watched her life force spray everywhere. Without a backward glance, the man sauntered off into the inky blackness of the night—and, then, I drifted off into the darkness of my own mind.

Bile burns at the back of my throat and tries to claw its way out at the memory.

"We need to call the police," I cry, coming out of my memory.

I clutch at the lapels of Jack's jacket, desperately trying to keep myself grounded.

"What happened, love?" he queries.

"A woman. . ." I start, the tears welling up in my eyes. "A woman across the street was. . . she was murdered!"

Instantly, Jude's up. He gives the others a significant look.

"I'll go check it out."

With that announcement, he turns around and marches up the steps out of the basement. No one says a word as Jack rocks me. My hiccupping sobs echo throughout the room. Sian and Elise come and place a gentle hand on my leg. Theo and Arthur pull their chairs over so that they can be closer to me. It doesn't take long for Jude to come running back inside, his clothes rumpled and askew.

Did he go to check on a dead woman or have a quickie?

"Sian—call the bizzies[1]," he barks. "Make it an anonymous tip. We have to get out of here now—it was a *Tertiary* attack."

At these words, everyone else jumps up in a panic. Jack all but dumps me on my feet, wrapping the blanket tighter around me.

"I'm confused," I mumble. "Who are the busies? And I thought the Tertiaries were the ones we were trying to gain respect from. . ."

Are the Tertiaries not the good guys, I wonder.

Did I get confused and they actually meant something completely else—like the Tershes are a gang?

Was the murder gang violence?!

I shiver at the thought—the *only* thing I want with a gang is to bang.

"There's no time for explanations," Arthur says gently. "We have to go now."

And that's how I ended up riding the train back to Oxford butt naked, wrapped in nothing but a blanket—*not* that anyone on campus will be surprised. I've marched back to my one-room apartment in less.

What *is* surprising is that all six of the others come with me.

The entire ride back to Oxford was rife with muttered words and anxiety. The four men huddled together to talk, look around, and whisper some more; Elise and Sian sat closely next to one another, afraid to even look around. I am still a bit in shock, so I don't even question when they follow me to my living quarters.

Here I'm about to bring six of the hottest people I've ever met home and it's not even to fuck—hell, I'm not even contemplating it!

I guess all I needed to be on the straight and sexless narrow was a little street murder with a dash of animorph mystery.

Chapter 11

Belle

I'm so distraught that, when I unlock the door to my apartment, I completely forget that I always have the place set up. . . *in case I bring somebody home.* The table to the left has two tea lights, a hot oil warmer, and anal beads hanging where someone else would probably hang their keys. Further into the room, you can see more objects meant for, ah, sexual pleasure.

I've been meaning to pick up and make the place a little bit more respectable, but I obviously didn't intend to use any of it—I mean, the warmer isn't on nor are the tea lights lit. I'm hoping that, given the circumstances, everyone just ignores what's around them. I lead them to my small living room area. Arthur takes a seat on my couch and yelps as he leaps back up.

Panicked, I cry, "What's wrong?"

I'm terrified that the murderer has somehow followed me home, got to my house before me, and the giant man is hiding in my child-sized couch.

Sounds legit as shit to me.

But, instead of my nightmare springing forth, Arthur reaches back a hand and pulls out a massive black cock.

"Oh, that's where that went," I exclaim. "I was looking for it the other night. . ."

I trail off when I notice that everyone is staring at me like I've grown a second head. Yeah, maybe I should have cleaned up first, but I wasn't expecting any company! I realize that I'm still standing there with the double-ended dildo. I drop it and kick it under my couch like a lady.

"Is anyone going to explain to me what happened now?" I ask, turning everyone's attention away from my clam stuffer to the problem at hand. "Are Tertiaries the good guys or the bad guys?"

I mean, they are going to have to work really hard to convince me that those dudes are the good guys—*considering I saw one of them slash a woman's throat out.*

Theo opens his mouth to speak but closes it; then, opens it again and closes it, like a fish out of water. He lifts up his hand and kind of gives a shrug.

"They're not good and they're not bad. They just. . . are," he says.

"That was a *terrible* explanation," I deadpan.

"What he means," Jude intervenes, ever the middleman, "is that they're in charge. They're the law. It doesn't matter if what they do is wrong."

A lightbulb goes off in my head.

The Tertiaries are part of law enforcement.

"Oh, so they're the corrupt cops," I mutter. "Why in the ever-living hell are we trying to gain the respect of people who are corrupt?"

"Because that's how society is built, love," Elise explains. "It's the powerful who are in charge and the weak who submit to them."

I cringe, but she's telling the truth. The dean of Oxford isn't top dog at the university because of his stellar academics—but because of his *name*. And the privilege and wealth that comes with that is hereditary, not something that you work towards.

"I still don't think we should condone murder," I frown.

"Aye, lass, I agree," Arthur nods, "but she was human. What can we do?"

"I. . . whaaa? What am I supposed to do with that explanation? If she had been a goat, would it have been any different?!"

"No," Jack answers matter-of-factly. "It definitely wouldn't have mattered if she were a goat as they're barely a Secondary."

I glare at his sarcasm.

"Don't be an ass! I know that!"

"Well, Tertiaries can't be arsed with humans."

"What does that even mean?" I screech.

"It means that they couldn't care less," Sian adds.

"What do they care about?" I snap angrily.

Theo shrugs again.

"Fellow apex hunters," he offers.

"These people sound like militant PETA! Screw squirrels—we only care if you're a ti—" I cut off. "A lion."

Tiger brings to memory the man's hand turning into a striped paw and slashing the woman's throat. I actively try to get the image out of my head by imagining my parents having sex. Funny how not even a couple hours ago I was trying to get *that image* out of my head—now, I gladly embrace it.

"Well, I hope some non-corrupt cops catch this fucker and put him in jail for life. Although," I add sourly, "they would have a lot more to go on if we could give them more than just a hit and run report!"

Because that's *exactly* what I feel happened. We basically are accomplices, not giving all the information—like hitting the car and running from the scene. Jack snorts.

"We'll be lucky if this is even mentioned in the news."

"I'm surprised they even left a body," Elise adds. "What kind of shifter was it?" she asks me.

Scarily enough, I know exactly what she means, but I want to keep pretending that it was just my imagination and that the man's hand didn't turn into a tiger paw—that he had used a knife to cut the woman's throat. It doesn't even cross my mind to ask how Sugar Tits, I mean, Elise knows.

"I didn't see anything but the woman and all the b-b-b-blood."

The tears begin to well in my eyes again and Sian places a comforting hand on my shoulder.

"Don't worry," she soothes.

I smile weakly at her, but in my brain I scoff.

Don't worry?!

Whoever—*whatever*—these people are, they're obviously into cannibalism.

Jesus.

First, my parents are sex freaks.

Then, I let Jack fuck my ass, even though I'm supposed to be celibate—butt fuck it. I refuse to get anal over this one small relapse.

And, now, I'm a witness to a murder by a man who might be an animal—and *not* in the sexy way.

Will the horrors never end?

Chapter 12

Theo

THE SLIPPERY DICK

"I need to use the restroom," Belle announces.

None of us say anything as she gets up and walks into the bathroom, firmly shutting the door behind her. A wooden sign clangs against it. I squint, reading the words:

GO AWAY—I'M BATIN'

I open my mouth and promptly shut it.

That can't possibly mean what I think. . . then again, she just drop-kicked a rubber John Thomas under her sofa—a sign about beating the bishop seems likely given the evidence.

"I think Belle's in shock," Jude whispers. "She just found out that one of her parents is a shifter and, then, saw another one kill an innocent woman."

"How do we know she was innocent?" Jack tosses out like the ass he is.

Jude gives him a sour look.

"Don't be a wanker," he snaps, and I laugh, pointing to

56

Belle's sign that the others hadn't seen.

"Is she. . . some kind of sexual pervert?" Arthur ventures in a hushed voice.

"I knew we liked her!" Sian crows.

"I didn't say that I didn't!" Arthur counters fiercely. "There's nothing wrong if she is!"

Jack chortles.

"Anyone that buff can pervert on me whenever," he grins, and Elise throws a pillow at his head.

"Maybe she's a high-end prozzy?" I offer.

Jack tips his head.

"Huh, maybe. . . she didn't charge *me* though—and buggery always cost more."

Elise throws *another* pillow at him.

"Stop rubbing it in that you got a leg over with her. Also, how do you know *that* costs more? Are you a curb crawler now?"

"It would make more sense if it were cheaper," Jude chimes in thoughtfully, and we all look at him askance. "What? Buggery never got a woman up the duff."

Before anyone can comment, there's a knock at the door. Instantly, we all tense. Jude immediately stands and marches over to the door, sniffing and peering out. After a second, he swings it open. An attractive older woman in a business suit stands there.

"Good evening," Jude tells her. "Belle is busy at the second, but she'll be right out."

From his stance, I know Jude is assessing the stranger. I can smell that she's human, but my senses aren't the best out of water. I'm pretty much the most useless shifter unless something disastrous happens at a swim party.

The tall woman places a hand on her hip.

"I'm here for Taco Tuesday—*what are you doing here?*" she demands almost rudely.

Ever the overly correct gentleman, Jude goes, "It's Thursday."

The woman narrows her eyes.

"I know that. It's a rain date," she snaps. "So, again—why are you here?"

"Ummmmm. . ." Jude mumbles, clearly at a loss. "There was an incident, and we're helping Belle. We didn't know she was having a. . . taco party."

"Well, it looks like a sausage fest to me!" the stranger snorts.

"What the fuck does that mean?" Jack demands, ever *not* the diplomat.

Arthur looks at me and I just shrug in confusion, but Elise and Sian are losing it on the couch. Just then, Belle comes out of the bathroom. She takes two steps, sees who's at the door, and rushes forward.

"Professor Yardley! I. . . I completely forgot about our plans," she confesses with a gorgeous blush.

The professor sniffs.

"Obviously! It looks like you're having an orgy!"

"N-n-no!" Belle stutters, looking at us wildly. "I've. . . renounced my ways. I have a problem—I can admit that now. These are my friends who are helping me. I can no longer indulge in *tacos.*"

The last part is said with absolute resignation, and I have no idea why she can't eat the American meal anymore. The Yardley woman raises one skeptical brow.

"Really—then, what are *those two* doing here?" she queries in a narky[1] tone, pointing at Elise and Sian.

"I swear I'm not tonguing their tacos!" Belle denies loudly.

From across the hall, there comes a groan.

"Dammit, the wee peng Yank isn't Aussie kissing anymore! What are we going to do on Tuesday nights, now?" the neighbor bloke moans to someone.

Everyone swivels to stare at Belle, who looks down and shuffles her feet nervously.

"I might have let my neighbors film me a time or two. . . or twenty. But who's counting? And, that's their major—so, really, I was helping them. But that was all in the past. I promise I haven't relapsed, unless you count Jack fucking my ass earlier. . ."

"Wow," Arthur breathes, and poor Belle looks close to tears.

"She's definitely a nympho," Sian stage-whispers to me.

"There's nothing wrong with that," I soothe, seeing Belle's downtrodden expression.

"I'm working on it," she mutters. "Sort of."

"We have bigger issues," Jude interjects, reminding me about the Tertiary attack.

"Ms. Harper, we will talk about this tomorrow," Professor Yardley huffs. "I want you in my office at 10:00 a.m. sharp."

"Yes, ma'am," Belle replies politely, cringing.

The professor gives Jude one last look of disgust and walks away. Ignoring the snotty woman, Jude shuts the door and turns to Belle.

"Don't worry, no one here is judging you," he assures her. "What I am concerned with is why a woman was murdered near where we hold our weekly meetings."

"You think it was a message?" Elise asks sharply.

"That's what I'm trying to figure out. Jack, Arthur, and I are going to go back to Banbury and investigate. Belle, can Theo, Sian, and Elise stay here with you?"

"Of course—I only have one room, though," she explains, hooking a thumb toward a closed door that, thankfully, doesn't have a wanking sign on it, too.

"I can sleep in the bath[2]," I offer.

One of the perks of being a small fish, I can easily fit inside one and swim around.

"Perfect," Jude praises, clapping a hand on my shoulder. "We'll be back."

With this, Jack, Arthur, and Jude depart. Elise and Sian take Belle and lead her to the sofa to sit. With slumped shoulders, I go to join them, trying not to feel too disheartened. I understand why Jude wanted me to stay behind —*what help can a water shifter be on land?*

Suddenly, Belle takes my hand and gives me a beautiful smile. She has been nothing but accepting of me and my slippery dick. With that thought, I stop crying stinking fish[3] —I can't change who I am.

I can only embrace it as she has.

Chapter 13

Belle

"I'm sorry about Professor Yardley," I start as soon as Theo sits down next to me.

He looks so. . . *disappointed*—I hope it's not with me. I bite my lip and fidget nervously when he runs a hand through his blond hair and sighs. Theo's crystal-clear blue eyes lock on mine, pinning me in place.

"It's as Jude said—you have nothing to explain or apologize for."

"I swear I forgot all about tonight's. . .ah, rendezvous."

In truth, I'm a little embarrassed. Between my relapse earlier and my teacher coming to my door, I doubt anyone takes my vow of celibacy seriously. I mean, I have bigger concerns, but still, SA hasn't cured my habit yet.

It's only your second meeting, I remind myself firmly. *Plus, you saw a woman get her throat ripped out, so I deserved that quickie with Jack. . .*

Even though it happened beforehand.

Semantics.

"No one is judging you for your preferences," Theo continues.

"That's right, love," Sian adds. "To each their own. Elise and I don't do dick—ever."

I gasp at this announcement.

"What do you mean you 'don't do dick'?"

"We're minge munchers, hun. We never ever add dick to the mix."

"You've never. . . *had dick*?!" I squawk incredulously.

"Nope, we're gold-star lesbians!" Sian crows proudly.

"Someone gave you a gold star for fucking other chicks?! How come no one's ever given me one?" I pout.

I scissor like a champ, thank you very much.

Elise and Sian both break out into peals of laughter.

"No, love," Sian hoots. "A gold-star lezzie is a woman who's never been with a man. Elise and I have been together for eight years."

She shoots Elise an affectionate look, smoldering with promise, and I cock my head to the side in thought.

"If you two are a couple. . . how does that work for the program?"

"Program?' Elise wonders.

"The meetings," I clarify. "I mean, how can you be together if. . ."

I trail off with a hand in the air, as if that conveys everything that I haven't said.

"Oh—I understand," Elise exclaims. "So, our society really frowns on my relationship with Sian, so we usually keep it hidden. Our parents know and don't acknowledge either one of us anymore."

My hand falls limply at her words—that hadn't been what I was asking *at all*, but fuck if it doesn't gut me. A sudden anger courses through my body.

"Fuck your parents and their pretentious rules. Do you two love each other?" I demand hotly.

"Abso-bloody-lutely," Sian grins. "As you said, she's my 'breast friend'."

"Then, screw what our society says about you two being together. I just meant I didn't know if you were breaking any rules of the meetings by being a couple."

"Nope," Theo supplies. "Like you, we accept everyone in the group for who and what they are. Elise and Sian came to us as a couple and remain that way."

Huh.

Interesting.

I guess as long as they only have vanilla sex once in a boring blue moon, it's cool—who knows what the rules are for them. I'm glad that it's a little more cut and dry for me. . .

Sort of.

I feel like every time I get one question answered, another pops up. I blame our society for sexualizing everything. I'm actually just looking for a scapegoat since *I* sexualize everything.

"Well, I promise that I wasn't going to stick my tongue in Professor Yardley's hot-box. Those days are over for me."

"That's a shame," Elise bemoans with a sly wink.

Um. . .

Was that a 'come join Sian and I in muffdiving later' wink?

I clear my throat, trying not to envision the three of us entwined, my mouth on someone's pussy and someone's on mine, while Theo jerks off watching.

"So, about the murder," I divert.

I need to turn my attention a.s.a.p. before I relapse again. *And again.*

"Jude and the others will try to learn as much as they can, but there's really nothing we can do about it. We're in danger simply because we know," Theo explains, and I shiver at his words.

I haven't even thought about it like that—how far will this murderer go to keep his killings hidden?

A dead woman's tongue can't wag—or lick vag.

Look at me rhyming in my panic.

"B-b-but the guy doesn't know I saw him, right?"

Theo gives me his patent shrug.

"I think if he caught a whiff of you, he would have turned around. I'm surprised he didn't. Tertiaries have fantastic senses—he must have been in a hurry."

"Yeah," I mutter. "Escaping the scene of his crime."

"Well, if he goes back to "check on things", he might catch our scent, then. We try to remain as innocuous as possible. We're the lowest men—and women—on the totem pole."

Just because we are sex addicts?!

Ugh.

How fucking ridiculous is that crap?

A damn murder is higher on the societal totem pole.

Society has its priorities more out of whack than that Hermione Granger.

Chapter 14
Belle

*D*ing.

Theo's phone pings an incoming message.

"It's Jude. They're on their way back—he says, 'don't leave Oxford'."

I breathe a sigh of relief.

"Thank goodness that they're ok." I stand up from the couch. "I guess I'd better get the rooms ready. I have some spare bedding and an extra blanket or two that I can bring out here for the guys. Sian, Elise, are you ok to share my single bed?"

I dial back my secret enthusiasm at my words and hope they came out a question as opposed to an eager suggestion.

"Actually," Sian says, "I have a cousin that lives right off campus. Elise and I can stay the night with her so we don't put you out."

Disappointment blooms within me, but it's probably for the best if we're all to remain *innocent*.

"Ok, that works," I respond with a fake smile on my face. "I'll just go get that bedding for the boys, then."

I step into my room and grimace. It's set up like a sexual predator's dungeon. On second thought, it's probably best that Elise and Sian are not spending the night. I kick my X-cross out of the way and kneel down in front of my dresser. I got that beauty from whipsandchainsonwheels.com—they make dominance mobile.

I root around in my drawer and have to throw out some feathered handcuffs, a cat-o-nine tail, and a pair of nipple clamps before I finally reach the extra sheets. I plan to use them to cover the couch—and my couch is probably the one you definitely want to have a sheet on.

Hopefully, none of the boys carries a blacklight in their pocket or my living room will look like Sex Crime Central.

When I finally find and gather everything, I scoop it all into my arms and go back out to the living room. The window is open wide and a nice breeze is blowing through. Theo is sitting by himself on the couch.

"Where did the girls go?" I wonder.

I notice that the bathroom door is wide open and the tub is running.

"They went over to Elise's cousin's already," Theo explains.

"Oh, I didn't get to say goodbye," I whisper with genuine disappointment.

"They didn't want to worry you. I think Elise is a little scared," Theo whispers back.

"Well, I can understand that—*I'm petrified, considering the circumstances.* Why is my window open? Are you hot?" I ask him.

"Oh, I completely forgot that the birds asked me to shut it."

"Birds?"

"Oh, it's slang for 'girls', but ironic considering, eh?"

"Oh, I see!" I say, finally understanding that Elise and Sian opened it.

"Yeah, they flew out it."

I turn to stare at Theo—*the British sure do take their slang to a different level.*

"What? They went out the window?!"

Theo just shrugs.

"Yeah, it's easier than the door, don't you think?"

"The door would have been less inconspicuous," I retort dryly.

"Than two birds flying out of it?" Theo laughs.

There's some more British idioms to confuse me.

"Right," I laugh, not wanting to seem like an American dolt.

Honestly, it's probably best that Sian and Elise have already left. To be truthful, I was having some seriously naughty thoughts of them—us—together.

Now, I'm temptation-free—except that's a lie because another yummy enticement is standing right in front of me —all six foot two, blond hair, green-eyed gloriousness of Theo.

There's an awkward pause while I try not to stare at his dick like it's an ice cream cone and I'm about to go on a sugar bender. I must not succeed very well because he asks me if I'm all right. I let out a nervous laugh.

"Er, yeah; everything's totally fine," I fib not smoothly at all. "Right, well, I'm just going to go maybe whip up some snack food for everyone. I bet you're all very hungry—I know I'm *starving*—"

I quickly shut my mouth before I say something stupid —like how I'm hangry for some ice cream dick.

"Ok. I'm going to my bath," Theo returns.

I nod and busy myself making some hors oeuvres,

reminding myself that is not pronounced 'whores'—which is a shame because I love to devour whores.

I hear the bathtub stop running and do my best not to envision Theo stripping and getting into the water.

I'm failing.

Is it strange that a man is taking a bath? I wonder, trying to divert my attention.

Maybe not here in the U.K.

Maybe British men like to have a leisurely soak. . .

I groan out loud at the thought of Theo in a bubble bath and all the bubbles popping slowly away, one by one.

"Son of a bitch!" I cry as I take something out of the oven and burn myself.

I was so busy daydreaming that I forgot to put on oven mitts. Hopping back on both my feet and trying to suppress tears, I run over to the kitchen sink, sticking my injured hand underneath the faucet. The cold liquid instantly soothes the burn.

"Damn it, Belle, get your head out of the gutter!"

I swear Karma is punishing me for my thoughts.

Opening up my freezer, I find a few more items that maybe the others would like to snack on, but I don't know what everyone likes. Jude, Arthur and Jack aren't here to ask, only Theo. I bet he would know what everyone likes, though, and I definitely need to ask since I don't want to be wasteful.

That's just an excuse for you to try to barge in on him naked so that you can see his cock, my mind snarks.

Shut up, brain, I snap right back. *Nobody wanted your opinion.*

Yeah! my thirsty vagina roars. *Nobody wanted your opinion!*

Fortified that I have my vagina's blessing to go see Theo in the buff, I march over to the bathroom door.

Because we don't want to waste food; no, siree.

There are people starving. . . not to mention my hippo's yawn is, too.

Chapter 15

Jude

THE COCKCHAFER

BEFORE

I zip ahead of Jack and Arthur, the wind lending me speed for once. It always seems as if I'm fighting the airflow, but tonight it's blowing north towards Banbury. I make the normally thirty-minute trip in seven—thanks to aerodynamics and straight-shooting it above the trees.

I land inconspicuously on the light pole near where the human woman was murdered. It's not working, an advantage the Tertiary used. The stench of blood permeates my senses, but the body has been removed—meaning, the shifter came back to clean his mess or, more likely, someone else did. This is confirmed when a jackal creeps out of the shadows, its muzzle stained red.

What better way to destroy evidence than by eating it?

I watch the creature warily, waiting for others to appear. Jackals are small, vicious Secondaries, but what makes them

70

dangerous is their ability to work in a pack. Surprisingly, though, no others join the one below me. I open my senses and know he is alone.

Interesting.

Who are you working for, Secondary?

I know for a fact that this shifter didn't kill the woman. Only an animal with large, powerful claws could do that kind of damage. Usually, shifters kept to their kind, barely even speaking to other Tiers—another reason our SA meetings are taboo. If it were only a group of cockchafers, that would be acceptable—*pathetic*, but still acceptable—but because it's a mixed group of Primaries, the shifter world would think we've lost the plot.

Not that it's anyone else's business.

Suddenly, the jackal looks up and narrows its gaze directly on me. The beast emits a low, feral growl in warning, telling me without words that he—or she—knows that I'm here. In response, a noxious-smelling gas begins to leak out of my body beyond my control. It's an instinctual defense tactic native to many insects and anything involuntary for the animal is hard for a shifter to act against.

I watch the plume of my own special brand of protection waft over the jackal, who yips and shakes its head side to side in an attempt to dislodge the foul scent. I fly down the road to a brown window ledge that will camouflage me well. I keep a wary eye on the jackal, mentally deciding whether I should follow it or rejoin Jack and Arthur, who are waiting for me outside of town.

The jackal makes my decision for me when it drifts into the shadows and shifts into his human form. He's a tall man, surprisingly so, with skin darker than midnight and eyes to match. The man steps back into the street, where he's briefly illuminated by a streetlight a few paces away from the broken one I was on.

Blood still smears his face—I can see the scarlet stain against the brilliant white of his teeth when he smiles threateningly.

His voice is a deep rumble, much like his animal's growl, when he shouts, "I smell you, bug. Watch it, or you might get smashed."

With that, he jumps back into the darkness and runs off, turning mid-pace back into his animal side. Since he had been naked, nothing impedes him, and I know he's going to a recce[1] spot to change. Shifters might be broken into a hierarchy of brute strength, but we all struggle with the same problems of going from creature to human and vice versa.

I need to leave before the guy brings back a pack of jackals and tries to make good on his word. I spread my wings and flap them experimentally, a buzzing sound coming from the movement. I get ready to leap into the night when the light beyond the window is turned on. Instantly and subconsciously, I fly towards it—smacking my small frame into the glass when I reach the barrier.

I hit it once...

Twice...

Thrice...

Internally, I fight the madness to get to the light. My brain understands all too well what's happening, but I can't gain control of my dumb animal. Shifting is actually very dangerous business. I can easily be blown into oncoming traffic and mowed down by a saloon or be eaten by a hungry bird. But, most likely, cockchafers are likely to be killed by their own instincts. This is why I try not to shift at night or near towns—people hang those lights meant to attract insects.

It's how we lost my dad's brother, Uncle Robin.

I'm just about to crash into the window, again, when a shadow comes marching in front of me. An elderly woman opens up the window brusquely and pokes her head out. With a rolled-up rag, she starts swiping at my form whilst screaming at the top of her voice[2]. I dodge her blows in a seemingly drunken fashion, half trying to evade her and half trying to slip past her to my death.

"That's it!" she screeches, shutting the window back firmly in place.

I heave a sigh of relief as I watch her hobble out of the room—except, she left the damn light on. I'm half-tempted to shift back into a human when her shadow comes back into view. I mentally shout in panic when I see that she's carrying a can of Doff[3].

Thankfully, her frail form blocks the bulb, and I'm broken from my light trance. I hastily flap my wings and fly off into the night away from the town and opposite the jackal, back towards Jack and Arthur.

Jack is still in his ass form, trotting back and forth where I left him with Arthur, south of Banbury. The Scott is in human form, dressed in jeans and a button-down that Jack carried on his back. I land softly on the grass and change back into a man before striding over to Jack and Arthur.

"We need to get out of here. Now. A Secondary ate the evidence—jackal."

Arthur doesn't need to be told twice. He strips without blinking, stuffing his clothes into the bag slung over Jack's back and shifts. He jumps up onto Jack and I follow suit shifting. Together, we zoom back to Oxford like there's something on our tail.

A jackal.

Chapter 16

Belle

Tap.

Tap.

Tap.

I lightly knock on the bathroom door but get no answer.

"Theo," I call softly.

No response.

I knock a little bit harder.

"Theo," I shout a little bit louder.

Still nothing.

I do this three or four more times before I finally bang down the damn door. I even scream before I remember my window's open. I quickly rush over and shut it; then, rush back to the bathroom, afraid that maybe Theo's passed out in the tub.

I turn the handle to find it unlocked and step inside because I'm saving his life—which is way more important than saving his privacy. But when I step into the bathroom, there's no Theo. It's just a tub. . .

With a fish.

It looks like the same fish that Theo sent me a picture of the other night.

Oh my God, did the British hunk bring his pet fish and put it in my tub?

How did Theo even manage that—does he hide it on him in a plastic bag? It's surely tiny enough. I stare at the thing in horror. Where the hell did Theo go?

I run out of the room crying his name.

I rush to my bedroom, but no Theo—I even check behind the door and in my closet.

Sprinting out, I smack right into his muscled chest. Theo's dripping wet all over my wooden floor. Strong arms band around me and catch me as I fall.

"Belle, are you ok?" he asks frantically.

"No!" I gasp. "I couldn't find you! I went into the bathroom. I called your name and you didn't answer!"

"I was in the bathroom the entire time," he says. "And I can't answer when I'm like that."

"What do you mean?" I snap.

There's *no way* Theo was in that bathroom unless he was behind the door...

But, even then, his frame is far too large to fit behind it.

"My fish can't speak under water," he explains.

I look at him like he's crazy.

That's it.

It's officially happened.

I found one of the sexiest men on earth and he's telling me that fish can't talk.

"Dude, I know fish can't talk! How did you even get your fish in there?"

Theo squints at me in confusion. I squint back until a knock at the door makes us both jump.

"Shit," Theo whispers. "Get behind me. I didn't hear from Jude that they were here."

I step behind him, plastering my chest to his back, and wrap my arms tightly around him in fear.

After a pause, Theo lets out a hushed chuckle.

"Belle," he whispers, "you're going to have to let go of me if you want me to go see who's at your door."

"Oh, sorry," I stammer, but I grasp onto him even harder, scared.

"It's ok. . . you can release my cock, now," he suddenly chokes out.

I realize that I've involuntarily wrapped my hands around the base of it.

"My bad," I wince.

His cock is standing completely at glorious attention, beads of water dripping off it from his bath. I want nothing more than to lick him dry. Theo clears his throat and steps away, peeping through the door. He must know the person on the other side because it swings open and in marches a naked Jude, followed by Arthur and Jack.

"I-I-I'm super tired," I breathe. "I think I'm going to tuck in."

"Are you feeling all right?" Theo asks in concern.

"Yep, right as rain. Just, ah, fill me up—I mean *in*— tomorrow," I say in a rush, before sprinting to my bedroom and slamming the door shut behind me. "Oh, and lock up, please!"

Phew.

Sex crisis averted.

Those four almost found themselves in an orgy and they didn't even know it.

At ten minutes to nine, I make my way to Professor Yardley's office. I want to make sure that I arrive early, so I don't get a tongue lashing. Normally, I would *love* to have a tongue lashing—*but now isn't the time.*

I cross campus brusquely, gazing sightlessly into the woods that circle around the parameter. Suddenly, some movement catches my eye, and I squint to see. It's some animal that I can't name—rather large—*and it's staring at me.*

Like, legit, it's homed in on me.

My feet stumble a bit at the intensity in the creature's gaze when I swear it fucking winks at me!

I repeat—it winked!

That. . . can't be right. It must have just blinked, but with one eye. Animals do that, right?

I quickly turn to run and trip in my haste. I look back, sure that the unknown beast is about to be upon me—*but it's gone*, and I wonder if my mind made up the whole thing. I finish walking to the building where Professor Yardley's office is and enter, slightly dazed.

Once inside, I shake my head to clear it and rehearse what I'm going to say to my literature professor as I stroll down the long hall to her corner office. My feet shuffle over the tweed-like texture of the carpet, and I swear it's made of the same material as the itchy cardigans the students and professors wear.

It's even the same puce color—set-off nicely by the yellowish walls.

Kind of like barf.

Good thing my appetite is already gone. I lost that a long time ago after talking with Jude and the others. I want to barf at what I've seen, but I know I need to keep it together.

This carpet doesn't need my help.

I run through the excuses in my head to give to my professor, but they all seem so trivial—considering everything that I talked about with Jude and the others last night.

When I reach Professor Yardley's door to her office, it's open; so, I waltz right in like I have in the past. The office is large, being situated in the back corner of the building, and Yardley's desk is beyond where I can see. It's not until I round the door jamb that I notice there are three men in the room.

Professor Yardley is sitting behind the elegant wooden desk, her face frozen in a dazed and confused expression—her eyes glazed and unseeing. The three men seem to startle when I suddenly appear, as if surprised that I just sauntered in.

"Hi," I mumble nervously.

The sound of my voice snaps Professor Yardley out of her trance.

"Oh, Miss Harper, I wasn't expecting you so soon," she frowns, a hand coming up to rub her temple.

"I'm early," I apologize. "I can step out."

I hitch a thumb behind me to indicate the direction I want to escape toward, as the room feels thick with tension.

"Oh, there is no need," the man in the middle says with a genial grin. "We were just wrapping up here."

Professor Yardley nods.

"Yes, we were. Dean Hardwick, this is Miss Harper. She is the foreign exchange student from the States, here on scholarship."

The dean of the university looks at me with keen interest. Normally, I would look back with the same interest—I mean, his name *is* Hardwick—if that's not an invitation to ride a stiff cock, I don't know what is.

Yet, there's something else going on here that I don't understand. The dean's eyes bore into mine as if he's trying to divine my secrets. I'm used to sexual interest, but that's not how he's staring at me. It's something else—*something unnerving.*

"So nice to meet you, Miss Harper," the dean says, extending his hand toward me.

I stare at the proffered palm apprehensively—I'm waiting for it to morph into a tiger paw. When claws and stripes do not appear, I hesitantly stick out my hand to shake his. Dean Hardwick's grasp is firm, and his eyes appear oddly *triumphant.*

"This is one of the top students in my class—in all her classes, I'm told," Professor Yardley continues.

"Excellent," Dean Hardwick crows, still holding my hand hostage. "I'm so glad that you are such an *asset* to the University of Oxford."

The way he emphasizes 'asset' raises my hackles.

It creeps me out beyond words—I'm definitely *not* going to try to wrangle these dudes into a foursome.

"Miss Harper, would you mind stopping by my office later on this afternoon—say two o'clock?"

My brain scrambles to think of some lie because I don't want to be alone in this man's office—ever.

"Er, I'm getting my vagina waxed at that time," I blurt out like an idiot.

Every brow in the room raises.

Professor Yardley chokes on her sip of coffee.

"I-I mean, I'm getting a massage *without* the happy ending."

I emphasize this in case anyone is now questioning my

proclivities. To my surprise, Dean Hardwick just throws back his head and laughs.

"Miss Harper, you don't have to explain. Perhaps we can schedule another time. What is your phone number? I will have my secretary call you."

For the first time in my entire existence, I don't want to give someone my phone number—I don't even want to meet them for a late-night rendezvous, or an afternoon rendezvous, or a two-am-booty-call rendezvous.

Instead of giving Dean Hardwick my cell phone, I give him the number to my dorm room. I cringe at my stupidity at telling the man where I live but, as dean, I assume he can easily learn that information, right?

"Well, I will leave you and Professor Yardley to it. Again, thank you for bringing such lovely talent to our beloved university."

With that, the dean turns around and walks out, the two other unintroduced men trailing behind them.

One gives me a wink on the way out, and it reminds me of the wild animal I saw before I came inside.

What the hell is happening?

My vag doesn't even quiver once in excitement.

Something is seriously off. You know how some people listen to their guts? Well, I do that, but with my pussy.

If my meat curtains don't want to conceal your tube steak or fish taco—*then, I don't trust you.*

"I. . . uh, forgot something that I needed to do," I tell Professor Yardley lamely.

"Get your cunt waxed?" she offers blandly.

"Like you don't already know it is," I deadpan right back.

She sighs.

"Raincheck?" I lie.

Professor Yardley gives me a piercing look.

"Only someone with your skills could offer a rain cheque, like their muff were a hot commodity."

"Well, considering the range and mastery of all my skills. . ." I drawl out teasingly. "Good-bye, Professor."

"See you *soon*, Miss Harper," she reminds.

I might be in more danger of being attacked by this woman than a man who can turn into a tiger. I give her a wan smile and beat a hasty retreat. The war has just begun with that one. Poor Professor Yardley got a taste of what Belle Harper's tongue can do.

And once you go me, that's all you'll fucking crave. . . I need a better rhyme to describe how awesome my sex skills are.

But that's a battle for another day. I have bigger worries right now—like why my beaver didn't break the damn and flood my panties when that guy winked at me, or why the dean seemed intrigued with me as a person, not a sexual object to be used for his dirtiest fantasies.

Things aren't adding up in my world.

I whip out my phone as I dash back to my apartment.

It's time to call an emergency meeting of the S.A.

Chapter 17

Belle

"Hey, little Yank, you having a party again? And by party, I mean—"

"Yes, I know what you mean. Orgy, right?" I supply drily for my neighbor from across the hall as I unlock my apartment door. "Not today, Greg," I sigh. "It's not even 11:00 in the morning. What would even give you that idea?"

Dumb question.

When has a party at my place never *not* turned into an orgy?

"Because there's six people inside your apartment."

His words bring me up short.

"They're six people in my apartment already? How do they get here so quickly? Erm, well, right," I say to Greg, realizing I'm talking mostly to myself. "Uh, we'll just try to keep it down."

My neighbor smirks—there's zero point in convincing the guy that there's not going to be any sexual activity. I just give Greg a little wave and open my door. Or try to—*it's locked.* I put in the key and go into the room.

Sure enough, there sits everyone from S.A.

"How did you all get into my apartment?" I cry in astonishment.

Theo tips his head toward my wall.

"Through the window, love."

What is it with these guys and them using my window?

Jude walks over and takes my hand leading me to my couch.

"What's wrong? You said it was an emergency—is everything all right?" he prompts.

I open my mouth to speak and, then, shut it, unsure how to express my emotions,

"I. . . I went to meet Professor Yardley and Dean Hardwick was there with a couple other men," I begin. "I got a really strange vibe from him—the dean, that is."

Jude leans back from where he's lounging on my couch and looks at me in assessment.

"What kind of 'strange vibe'?" he prods.

I lower my voice to a scandalized whisper.

"Like he was *interested* in me."

Sian and Elise exchange a glance.

"Interested?" they ask together.

"Yeah, *interested* but *not* interested—if you know what I mean."

Theo lets out a bark of laughter.

"No, love, we *don't* know what you mean. We never know what you mean. Can you please clarify?"

I heave a sigh.

"I mean Dean Hardwick wasn't interested in me *sexually*. He kept staring at me like I was some interesting. . . uh, I don't know, *thing* to him! I have no idea how to express it, guys—and gals," I add for Sian and Elise. "But, I can tell that there wasn't any *other* interest—at least, the interest I'm used to getting."

"Does that disappoint you?" Jude asks, assuming the role of the group therapist.

I ponder his question for a moment.

"No," I finally answer, "not really. The dean kind of gave me the heebie jeebies. Honestly, last night's events have wiped any thoughts of hanky panky from my mind. . . well, mostly. It's a real mood killer—murder and all that. I know it doesn't probably seem like I'm trying very hard not to be a nympho, but I swear I'm working on it. But today, I promise you, it's the furthest thing from my mind!"

The others give me a bizarre look.

"A nympho" Jack repeats.

"Yeah, ya know—you be a nympho; I be a nympho. . . you guys don't know Fifty-Cent?"

From their clueless expressions, it tells me that they have no idea to what I'm referring.

"Never mind. Back to my problem. . ." I trail off, wondering if I seem absurd to them. "You know what? I don't know why I called you all here. I'm really sorry—I'm sure I've pulled you from your jobs and—"

I stop talking, flustered, realizing I probably have been a very big inconvenience to them.

"I'm sorry," I apologize again. "How rude of me to never even ask what any of you do in the day—do you have jobs? Do you go to school?" I wonder before addressing Theo. "Like, what do you do? I imagine something with marine animals, maybe?"

The smokin' hot blond frowns as if I've offended him, and I quickly scramble to backtrack.

"I-I mean, I just figured you did something with. . . with fish—because of your fish," I stutter in explanation.

Everyone else is looking at me with kind of a shocked expression, and I'm not sure what has gone awry in this conversation. Again, I attempt to clarify.

"Last night, Theo brought his fish over—popped him right into my tub—and I just figured anyone who brings their pet fish with them everywhere must love fish and work with them."

Arthur gives me the weirdest look.

"That wasn't Theo's pet fish—he doesn't even have one," the Scottish man says.

"Yes, he does!" I defend. "I know what I saw in my tub last night."

Theo throws up his arms in vexation.

"For the last time—that was me!"

I throw a decorative pillow at him from where I sit on my couch.

"What do you mean that was you?" I demand while Theo dodges my soft missiles.

He shoots me an exasperated eye roll.

"I'm a *slippery dick*."

"Listen—any other day, I'd jump on that, but now is not the time—"

Theo cuts me off.

"It's a type of fish."

"What's a type of fish?" I sputter.

Everyone appears just as baffled as I am. Sian lays a hand on my knee.

"A slippery dick is a type of fish. It's its name—just like a tit is a type of bird."

I sit back on the couch and shut my mouth. I literally have no idea what these people are talking about now. I squint, as if that will help their words make sense, but it just brings the room out of focus. I open my eyes back up fully. I might as well enjoy the eye candy that this group gives me if I'm not going to understand a lick of what they're saying.

"It's how we got into your room," Elise explains.

"Even though it's pretty hard for boobies to fly!" Sian jokes.

"Yeah, well, I had my ass hanging out the window, so I don't want to hear it," Jack snaps and his words bring a visceral image to mind. "I don't even want to think about all the people that saw my hairy bum."

"You guys—and gals—could have just waited and called me! I would have come right over. I don't know how you got here so quickly if you were all in Banbury," I mutter, mostly to myself.

"Well, I flew," Jude responds nonchalantly.

My mind boggles.

"You *flew* here?!"

Is this guy super rich or something?

Did he have a helicopter that could land on campus?

Why did he have to be rich and super good-looking?!

I toss my hands up in frustration.

"Don't you ever use your cat to get somewhere quicker?" Jude wonders, and I snort.

"Dude, the only place my pussy has helped me "get somewhere quicker" is in jobs. I have no problem climbing that corporate ladder one rung at a time, but *I swear* I'm not doing that here at Oxford!"

There's another moment of awkward silence, and I mentally cringe at admitting to fucking for better paying jobs.

"Um, all right," Arthur says after a beat. "Well, let's get back to why we're here. If you say you have a strange vibe from this guy, then we should listen to it because your feline instincts are probably accurate."

By "feline instincts", does he mean my *womanly instincts*?

"Erm, I guess I never thought about my, ah, feline instincts, but ok, sure. My feline instincts are telling me that the dean is *super* creepy."

"And to clarify," Jack adds, "it's because Dean Hardwick doesn't want to sleep with you?"

"No! I mean, kind of. It's like everyone isn't interested in me sexually since I've joined S.A." I pout. "I know that's for the best, but the guy could have pretended to be a little interested in my pussy. Instead, he was all 'creepo interested'."

Jack just shakes his head.

"Oh! And I almost completely forgot! Before all this—on my way to Professor Yardley's office—I saw this. . . *thing* watching me! I swear on my soul that it winked at me!"

"A thing? What thing?" Jack asks.

"An animal," I elucidate. "I think it was a fox, maybe."

Theo raises a brow.

"You don't know?"

I mirror the look he's giving me.

"Why would *I* know? I'm not an animalist, er, zoologist."

Jude glances at me.

"Well, most of us can recognize animals; although, sometimes we only can recognize our own kind," he adds like I'm slow.

I gasp.

"Did you just call me a pussy?! Like, because I have a vagina, I can only recognize other women?" Jude's mouth drops open at my words. "That's misogynistic!"

"N-n-no," he stammers, "because you're a cat."

"Like a 'cool cat'—huh, I *am* pretty cool," I say mostly to myself.

I realize that the conversation has degenerated into general confusion again amongst us.

"Was it a jackal?" Jude prods, getting things back on course.

"Do they look like foxes?" I ponder.

Arthur lets out an inarticulate grumble.

"Kind of—but not really. How can you not recognize animals?" he asks gruffly.

I shrug helplessly.

"I don't know. I don't go to the zoo very often."

Elise clucks at this.

"Well! I would hope not! They're the bane of our existence—some of *us* get trapped there!" she whispers in disgust.

I glance over at her.

Who the fuck gets trapped at a zoo?

Does she mean that sex addicts were having sex at the zoo, and they get stuck there?

Well, that puts a new spin on 'you and me baby ain't nothing but mammals because, clearly, they're doing it like they do on the Discovery Channel—*but at the zoo.*

"Yeah," Sian nods, "zoos are like pets—and you know how we feel about *that*. We don't have pets."

"Er, *I* don't have a pet, but *Theo* does. He has his fish!" I accuse.

Theo paces in agitation.

"For the last time, that's me!"

"Why do you keep saying that?" I screech right back.

"Because I'm the fish!" Theo yells, his clear green eyes bulging.

His blond hair flops over his forehead, and he looks a bit manic. I realize the guy is totally hot but, perhaps, crazy.

And, then, I think about my first time in S.A. and everyone roasting themselves.

Maybe Theo just equates himself to a fish.

Maybe he needs to accept himself as a minnow in a sea of big tuna—just like I need to accept Dean Stiffdick might not be interested in my stateside snapper.

"You're the fish—you're totally the fish," I soothe with a smile of understanding.

I feel like, for once, there's transparency in our words.

Chapter 18

Arthur
THE HORNY TOAD

"She's a nutter—buff[1] as fuck and sweet—but an absolute nutter," Sian giggles when Belle excuses herself to use the loo.

"Shhhhh!" Theo hushes. "She is not... well, *maybe...*"

Jack brays with suppressed laughter, but Jude just frowns.

"I think she's overwhelmed by everything and suppressing her emotions," he hypothesizes.

"I agree," throwing my two cents. "She didn't even ask what we discovered last night. I think she's scared and deflecting. The lass needs space, but to also feel safe."

"Quite the pickle. Arthur, why don't you stay with Belle tonight? The birds can stay with Sian's cousin to be close, and the rest of us can go back to Banbury. Maybe you can get her to open up and talk," Jude suggests.

I nod.

"Stellar idea—one of us definitely needs to stay, but

some space might do her some good. I will do my best," I promise.

Elise and Sian get up to leave.

"Tell Belle we said 'ciao' and we used her *door*," Sian jokes. "The Yank seems really put off when we use the window."

"We'll be back tomorrow for breakfast, if she's keen," Elise adds.

"That's a good idea—we can all reconvene here tomorrow for some nosh. Then, we can see if Arthur has learned what is bothering Belle most."

Now, I swallow—*maybe I'm not the best person for this job.*

"Jude, I think you should—"

"You've got this," he reassures me.

"Good luck, mate," Theo whispers as he follows the girls out of Belle's flat.

Jude claps a hand on my shoulder in passing, but Jack just smirks.

Belle comes out a few minutes later.

"Did everyone leave without saying good-bye *again*?" she whinges[2].

"We all thought you might be overwhelmed and could use some space," I explain.

She cocks her head to the side.

"Then, why are you here?" she asks in a purr that makes me nervous.

Her tone isn't accusatory—*it's sensual.*

"I, er, Jude that is, thought you might feel safer with someone around; so, one of us stayed."

"You volunteered?" she grins.

Not exactly—but I can't likely tell her that.

"Happily," I respond.

"Mmm," Belle hums. "And do you have any plans for *us*?"

"Um. . . sometimes I let my horny toad run free, if you wanted to let your cat out for a bit—but don't maul me, please," I joke.

Belle's grin widens like a shark's when it scents blood in the water.

"I smell what you're steppin' in—if you're feelin' froggy, jump, right?"

"Er, right," I agree apprehensively.

Suddenly, she lunges forward and leaps into my arms. I barely have enough time to register what's happening when she glues her lips to mine and wraps her long legs around my mid-section.

"I won't let my pussy maul you if you promise to pet it nicely," Belle growls.

I almost drop her.

Luckily, the lass seems to be doing most of the work holding herself up.

"Where do you wanna fuck me?" she demands.

My mind blanks.

"Everywhere," my mouth speaks without permission, eliciting a delighted laugh from Belle.

"Perfect," she murmurs. "Let's start in the kitchen, on the counters, with your head between my legs. From there, we can work through every room in a different position."

"H-h-how many positions are there?" I stammer like a virgin.

"Well, I've got three holes, two hands, and a lot of stamina—not to mention fucking in between my cleavage and ass cheeks. . . lot of possibilities. Aren't you glad you stayed to protect me?" she giggles.

I'd answer but my tongue is lolling outside of my mouth, and I've lost all control of it.

"That's the spirit!" Belle crows. "Quick—to the kitchen so we can put that thing to use!"

I follow the direction of her pointed finger and enter into the small kitchen. The counter barely has enough room for her to sit, but I place her delicately on top where she's directed.

The forward woman doesn't bat an eyelash when she whips off her top and bottoms. Her pants[3] quickly follow until she's just in a lacey red bra.

She spreads her legs wider than a dancer and pokes herself[4]!

My knees buckle at this raw display of sex; they crack against the floor hard, but I barely notice the sting—I can't take my eyes off the pink perfection of Belle's fanny.

It's bare and glistening with her juices.

"Come use that talented tongue on me," she urges.

I stare up into her blue eyes before answering.

"I can't," I confess. "I think I swallowed it."

Belle tosses back her head and shakes with laughter. The movement causes her tits to bounce up and dance. I'm utterly transfixed. She holds out a hand when she finally calms down, and I take it.

The lovely cat shifter yanks me forward between her legs. I awkwardly angle my mouth to give her an Aussie snog, but feel self-conscious—*what if I don't do it right?*

What if she hates it?

What if I can't make her peak?

"Stop thinking," Belle whispers, forcing my head closer. "I love it already."

"I haven't done anything," I smirk.

"Exactly," she parries.

It's enough to put me at ease, and I set to work.

I tentatively lick her soft folds, the wetness coating the tip of my tongue. She mewls hungrily, and I lap deeper—harder. This seems to be what Belle craves because she rocks her hips forcefully to meet my mouth.

I fuck her quim with my tongue like it's my cock, enjoying the taste of this beautiful woman. Her fingers dance across her bean, working herself into a state of frenzied lust.

Until she explodes.

Droplets of liquid splash across my lips and chin, and I lean back, startled. No woman has ever came like *that* for me before. The taste of her is intoxicating, but I don't get a chance to enjoy it because she pulls me up to her—*and licks herself off my face.*

"Yum," she groans in bliss. "Now, take off your pants and fuck me. Pretend I'm the kitchen help you caught fingering herself instead of working. Punish me with your dick —hard."

My hands unconsciously undo my belt while I gape at her.

What is this crazy Yank into?

"Oh, and don't forget to choke me," she adds.

I stop thinking after that and just do. It takes seconds for me to strip. I don't worry about protection—Belle's a cat and I'm a toad. It's not like I can impregnate her or anything, and shifters can't get STDs—but Belle might prefer it, regardless.

Clearing my throat, I admit, "I don't have any condoms."

"No worries. We're good," she promises.

It's all I need to hear.

Like a man possessed, I tackle her back further onto the counter and stuff her full. Belle releases a long low moan, and I fear that I've hurt her until I remember her last words to choke her...

Picking up my pace, I grip her hips hard and forcefully slam into her tight minge. Belle clings to my shoulders, and her cries of delight echo around us. I remember her words and release her hips to carefully wrap my hands around her throat.

"Squeeze," she directs.

At first, I hesitate, but gradually begin testing her threshold for pain—*it's high*...

And I like it.

A lot.

I've never done anything like this with a woman, and it sends me to new heights. Within minutes, I'm dancing the edge between holding back and busting a nut.

"God, yes, Arthur," she pants. "Come inside my pussy."

My knob must have a direct line of communication with this woman—and it obeys her every command.

I explode deep inside Belle's quim.

"Shit, I'm sorry. I didn't mean—"

"Arthur," she gasps, "that was. . . amazing—perfect amount of pressure. I fucking loved it."

"But. . . you didn't, ah, *you know*, did you?"

"Come? No, but I did before—*by your tongue*. Besides, this was just the first room, remember?" she adds with a wink.

I remember—*and I make a mental note to thank Jude for convincing me to stay.*

Chapter 19

Belle

*I*n the middle of the night, I get up to go get a drink of water because I'm dehydrated—not nearly as dehydrated as Arthur is, I assume, because he's the one who lost a whole bunch of bodily fluids. . .

If you catch my drift.

You would think that since it was me who took in all those bodily fluids, my thirst would be quenched—but I'm still parched—for an actual drink and more jizz. I think my brief stint of abstinence has sent my body into baby batter withdrawals.

Poor thing is used to a daily sperm shot.

I silently pad out of my bedroom, shutting the door shut softly behind me, before making my way to the kitchen. I grab a glass of water and guzzle it down like that lady I'm *not*. Liquid drips down my chin, a là Napoleon Dynamite, and I carelessly wipe them off with the back of my arm.

Stepping back out into my living room, which is softly lit with fairy lights, I stare out. The room's ambience is almost magical but, then again, I'm a whimsical whore. Not really looking at anything in particular—as I'm still half asleep—I swear to God I see fingers tapping on the outside of my window.

In horror, I watch as they wiggle the glass pane open. With zero hesitation, I whip my phone from my sleep short pockets and dial Campus Security. It rings once, twice, three times and, by now, my window is up nearly half a foot.

But what happens next is some Grade A bullshit.

Instead of a *human* hand creeping through my window followed by a human body that it's attached to—because that's how human hands work—a fucking monster crawls through my window and drops down into my apartment.

And by "fucking monster", I mean *a spider the size of a fricking dinner plate*!

A silent scream catches in my throat, and I drop my phone in absolute terror. The thing is big and hairy, and a newspaper is *not* going to do the job. The giant fucker looks like a tarantula on roids.

The spider demon lands silently on my floor, but I can feel the heavy vibration of it falling down. It twitches and all its hair seems to raise—just like the ones on the back of my neck.

I look around and see the little bookstand resting right at my feet between the bathroom and kitchen doors. Whipping off the decorative tablecloth that's covering it, I reveal a box full of sex toys. Grabbing a handful of bullet vibes, I throw them at the furry menace.

At first, it startles and scurries back, but then it turns its eight beady eyes on me and focuses—*like it knows who I am and what I'm up to.*

. . .

I realize that the small dogs *aren't* going to cut it, so I whip out the big ones—*a.k.a. the dildos.* I kiss one briefly before lobbing it at the spider tyrant. The eight-legged beast doesn't even flinch and just scuddles out of the way.

Oh my God—it has depth perception!

It's quick, agile, and deadly. There's no way it's not a killer, and I realize that I'll just have to end its life before it ends mine first. I'm also seriously regretting not buying that flamethrower—that would have come in handy right now.

Suddenly, it jumps—fucking jumps—on top of my coffee table—*like it's a kangaroo!* It rears back on its hind legs and stands.

"AHHHH!" I shriek, and it lets out a feral hiss.

That's it—I'm not convinced this thing isn't actually a cat.

Reaching blindly down into my toy box, I feel around for my double-ended black mammoth. I kiss the tip for good luck—because it's ok to go ass to mouth—and rear back before launching my raunchy silicone joystick.

I throw it as hard as I can, and sucker punch the tarantula right in its solar plexus—*that is, if spider's have a solar plexus.*

"Ha!" a yell in triumph before spinning around and running back into my kitchen.

I grab as many knives as I can and dash back. The tarantula's still trying to get off its back. It looks like a helpless beetle and the thought makes me shudder—those assholes are just as creepy.

I throw five steak knives all at once and miss—*all at once.* In my left hand, I still hold a butcher's knife. By now, the spider's flipped over, and it understands that I'm out for blood.

It comes running at me, and I ninja-chuck the knife at

the fucker. The blade catches him on one of its many legs and, instead of lopping it right off, the knife pins the bastard to my wood floor. The thing is only five feet from me now, and I let out another indelicate scream before rushing back to my bedroom.

"Arthur! Wake up!" I shout, flipping the sleeping man off my bed.

The poor guy has *no* idea what's going on as I grab a giant blanket to throw over the tarantula—to trap it.

I return to the living room but, instead of seeing the eight-legged nightmare pinned to the floor, it's a naked human. The dude is writhing in pain and one of his fingers is cut off. He's bleeding everywhere, and I finally connect the dots.

This bastard is like the tiger that killed the woman.

Chapter 20

Belle

*D*ick flapping and balls slapping, Arthur finally comes dashing out. He seems confused as to why there's a naked man in my living room, but I don't have time for questions. I run up and kick the spidey intruder. The man groans—*Arthur continues to stare in bafflement.*

"Go get help!" I screech at the redheaded man.

He finally blinks before dashing out my front door— buck naked.

Sweet Lord, I highly doubt anyone even blinks any more.

Realizing that I'm now alone with a wounded trespasser, I grabbed my double-ended dildo—because it clearly is a cock saver—and I start smacking the animorph intrude across his back and head.

"Ouch! Fuck! Stop! Hey! God damn it!" he curses, but I don't let up—I swing my black beauty like it's a bat.

"Take that, you. . . *whatever you are!*" I scream like a warrior woman.

The guy whirls around to me, his face lit with rage—*and then I see the fur pop out of his skin.*

And I know—*I know*—he's going to change into that *thing* again.

Not today, Satan!

I rear back with my dildo and slap him across the face as hard as I can with it. *And damn if my pimp hand ain't strong.* The spider jerk stumbles back, trips over the coffee table, smacks his head on the edge, and knocks himself clean unconscious.

I stand there, unsure of what to do, before I sprint over and kick him in the gonads—*again.*

You know that rule about kicking them when they're down?

I obviously don't have a problem with it.

I quickly go to the tiny hall closet and pull out a thing of *good old duct tape.*

It takes me less than seven minutes to completely tie this guy up until he's completely bound.

Do not underestimate the skills of a super freak—a sex addict is into all kinds of crazy shit.

Suddenly, there's a knock at my door. I swing it open without thinking because I assume it's Arthur. It's not—it's campus security, who I called and, then, hung up.

Well, I didn't *technically* hang up on him—I dropped my phone in panic when a tarantula crawled through my window.

Big difference.

"Ummmm..." I stammer.

"You called security, ma'am?" the guy on the left asks.

"Yes. I thought somebody was breaking in my house but, it turns out, they were...not."

I trail off, trying not cringe at my lame excuse.

The men attempt to step into my apartment, but I bar them. They can't see anything except for spidey's two feet—

which are wrapped in duct tape. I suppose I should be thankful that he's only sporting two instead of eight right now.

"I forgot that I was having a sex party," I hastily explain.

This brings the two security men up short.

"A sex party?" the one on the left speaks again.

"Yes, it. . . slipped my mind that I. . . asked somebody to break into my apartment and attempt to touch me because. . . umm, you know, I get my jollies off to that shit."

The guy on the right looks interested, but the other on the left just scowls

"Ma'am, rape is a very serious thing! That is no joking matter," he scolds sternly.

"No, no, no, you're mistaken," I start before slamming my hands on my hips. "Wait just a minute! Don't you kink shame me! You can't tell me what to do or how to feel!"

I take a breath, gearing up to give them the sex talk of their lives, when the door across the hall opens. It's my gamer neighbors. Thankfully, they've reminded me of my purpose.

"Hey, Wes," my neighbor says to one of the guards, "This is the Yank I was telling you about!"

"Oh," he says, "this is the super freaky slapper."

"Yeah, and when she says she's tying someone up, it's cool—they're really just having kinky sex."

"All right. But please know that we take campus security very seriously, ma'am," the guy directs at me.

I almost snort considering how half the time I see them sitting around fiddling on their phones. But I suppose it's reassuring that they came to my apartment when I called.

"Right. My apologies, I will not call security again for my forgotten sexcapades."

"We appreciate it. Maybe look into keeping a sexcapade calendar," the other guard offers unhelpfully.

With that, they march off and I quickly go back into my apartment.

Alone—with a naked man that can turn into a giant tarantula.

Where the hell did Arthur go?!

Chapter 21

Jack

THE ASS

At a quarter past two in the morning, there's a knock at my door. I quickly throw on some boxers and go answer it. On the other side stands Arthur—starkers.

"I hopped here as fast as I could," he pants.

"You hopped from Oxford to Banbury in the middle of the night? Are you barmy[1]?!"

All Primaries know not to go out at night. If you're the lowest level of shifter, it's a good way to get eaten or mauled to death.

"It's Belle, she's in danger! There's a shifter in the room with her. She woke me to go get help—I-I-I don't know what happened," he stutters in his haste to spit out his words.

"You left her alone with an unknown shifter?!" I growl at him. "Get on. We're running back."

I quickly shuck off my pants and shift into my ass. Arthur shifts, too, and hops onto my back. Together we race back to Oxford.

In my urgency, I mow down two security guards who yell

in dismay and fright, but I ignore them and keep going, not even concerned. I don't even shift when I get to Belle's flat, until I realize I can't open the door.

Awkwardly, I throw Arthur off my back and change. Arthur does the same. Both of us are starkers because I forgot clothing, but neither of us care. Panting, we sprint up to Belle's room and enter without knocking.

"Finally!" she screeches the minute we come into view. "I've been waiting for ages for you guys! I've had to pretend that it's a sex party in here—*not that anyone would question that.*"

Considering the amount of naked knobs in here, I can understand that. I walk over to the shifter that Belle has miraculously detained. . . *via duct tape.* The guy is unconscious, and I'm impressed.

"He-he-he-he-he-he turns into a tarantula!" the pretty Yank stutters in fright.

"What kind?" Arthur asks studiously.

Belle gives him a look.

"The big kind! How the fuck do I know?"

"You don't know what kind of tarantula he is?" Arthur presses.

"No!" she shrieks back.

Arthur looks over at me.

"Well, there's a good chance that he's a Tertiary, given their size and ability. There's only a few Secondary tarantulas out there."

"This one was as big as a dinner plate!" Belle adds with a shudder.

"Then, he's likely the Goliath bird-eating tarantula. Perhaps the giant huntsman spider," Arthur postulates.

"I'm sorry. What?" Belle frowns.

Arthur repeats himself.

"They're the largest species of tarantula on the face of the earth," I tack on.

"Are they poisonous?" Belle wonders.

"No, because poison is something that you ingest, but all tarantulas have some form of venom—that is, they are venomous and inject it through their fangs," Arthur responds.

Belle snarls and goes over to kick the unconscious man. I'm torn between laughing and groaning. Instead, I just swipe a hand over my face.

"What happened?" I demand.

"Well," she starts, "I got up to get a drink—to replenish my fluids because Arthur is *no* minute man—and, all of a sudden, I thought I saw a hand open my window. Except, it wasn't a hand—it was a tarantula! So, I started throwing some, ah, *toys* at him. Also, some kitchen knives. I ended up cutting off one of his furry legs. When I came back out after getting Arthur to throw a blanket on the thing. . . it was a *man,* and he was missing a finger. It's over in the corner of my living room and, as you can see, there's blood everywhere."

At this, Belle breaks down sobbing, her brilliant hair creating a veil over her face.

Arthur and I do our best to calm her, but it's obvious she's very distraught—not that I can blame her.

"We need to get this shifter somewhere else. We're going to be in trouble when he wakes up." I tell Arthur.

"Noted," he agrees.

"Do you have a car?" I ask Belle.

"No, I don't have a license in this country—I mean, that hasn't stopped me from driving on the wrong side of the road here, I just don't have one. *But* I can borrow one from a friend, maybe."

"Let's hope so because I can't haul him on my back," I say, nodding toward the unconscious shifter.

Belle quickly goes across to her neighbors and knocks on the door.

"Hold on! We've got to finish up this round!" someone yells from across the hall.

Belle stands there patiently while Arthur goes back to her room and gets dressed. He even brings back a pair of boxers for me.

"Sorry, mate. The best I could do," he offers.

I cringe as I slip his Y-fronts[2] on.

The neighbors finally open their door to speak with Belle. There's some quibbling and some promises made filming her getting a leg over[3] that I don't even want to begin to think about, but she comes back with car keys in hand.

"Let's go," Belle chirps.

Between Arthur and myself, we hoist the Tertiary onto our shoulders. We attempt to slip out of the flat as inconspicuously as possible and somehow manage to chuck the shifter into the back of the neighbor's truck.

Belle slips into the cab and Arthur climbs up beside her, shutting the door. I take the keys and drive. It's a silent ride as we go back up to Banbury except for Arthur texting everyone to meet us at the church.

"We're making a lot of emergency S.A. meetings," Belle observes. "And not the kind I hoped for."

Arthur shoots me a look and I just shrug.

How the Hell should I know what kind the woman hopes for?

"Sian and Elise are still with a friend. So, only Theo and Jude will be joining us," Arthur announces.

I glance at my rearview mirror to make sure the Tertiary is still asleep. I step on the gas, just in case, and arrive in

Banbury in record time. Jude is already at the Anglican church, waiting.

"What happened?" Jude demands.

"Let's just wait for Theo," I respond.

Belle is pacing around furiously and trembling like a leaf. She's clearly terrified at this secondary attack that she's witnessed.

The question—why do the Tertiaries want Belle?

Chapter 22

Belle

My worst nightmares have been actualized —*humans can turn into creepy crawlers and enter my room when I'm sleeping.*

Ok, I suppose I've never had a nightmare of a man turning into a tarantula and coming into my apartment that I battle like a boss bitch with dildos and knives.

But still.

I promise that you would be shitting yourself, too, right now.

Pacing furiously back and forth, I shove a hand through my colorful hair that's in complete and utter sexy disarray from my time earlier with Arthur.

I look over at him.

Jack and Jude are watching me, too—with worried looks on their faces. They *should* be worried. People are turning into gargantuan spiders. Jude looks thoughtful as well as concerned, but I catch him gazing at my long golden legs.

I toss him a wink.

It might be the end of the world, but I'm still DTF.

Theo comes barreling down the church stairs to the basement where we meet, looking ready to brawl. It's interesting to see the violence simmering in his eyes considering that he's not a very large or overtly aggressive man.

"Where's the shifter?" Theo demands in a voice that I never would have attributed to him.

Jude's staring at Theo with the same kind of wonder as me.

"Out in the truck that Jack, Arthur and Belle used to drive over here."

"Let's bring him down. Now."

"N-n-n-no!" I stutter. "That guy turns into spiderman! He's a dickhead Peter Parker!"

"It's ok, Belle," Arthur tries to soothe. "We'll be right back."

"I'll do a perimeter check while you three bring in the Tertiary," Jude directs.

I make a face.

A higher society fuck can turn into an animal?

The more I learn about these people, the less I want their respect—*or anything to do with them.*

Jack, Arthur, and Theo come back carrying Spidey between them as if the beefcake freak weighs nothing. To be fair, all three guys are packing some muscles under their shirts.

It's enough to perk up any dried up and terrorized vagina—and trust me—my jelly roll is horrified.

My muscle men toss the unconscious dude into a corner of the room, but I'm sure to keep a safe distance and a wary eye on him.

Jude finally returns, eyeing Eight-legs—correction, Seven-legs—with the same cagy expression as the others.

"I didn't smell anything—or see anything—and I flew over the area to check," he announces.

"Dude—where do you keep a plane around here that you can just fly" I snap.

Jude squints at me for a hard minute.

I squint right back in the same confusion when suddenly astonishment leaches onto his face. He blinks in an absolute shock.

"You do know that a cockchafer's a type of bug that has wings and can fly, right?"

Now, I blink at him.

"That's. . . very odd information to give me at this time; I did *not* know that. But what the fuck does a cockchafer have to do with anything?"

Jude clears his throat.

"It's a type of beetle—and that's what I turn into."

I take a giant ass step back.

And another.

Jude holds out his hands to show that he's absolutely no threat, but I'm ninety-nine percent sure this dude just told me that *he turns into animals like those other things I saw.*

"I'm a cockchafer," Jude repeats. "I shift into a beetle."

Jack looks at me sharply.

"And I'm an ass—I shift into a donkey. Theo's a slippery dick—a type of fish—and Arthur's a horny toad."

"And you're a cat," the Scottish man adds in his deep brogue.

I shake my head and start waving my hands in front of me in the common sign of negation.

"No, no, no, no, no!" I refute.

It dawns on me that these lunatics think that I'm some kind of animal shifter, too—apparently a kittycat.

Oh, my God.

How could our conversations have gone this far awry?

And why were they having Sex Anonymous meetings?

I have no idea what's going on, but it seems that Jude does. He's looking at me like I'm an interesting puzzle.

"We have a problem on our hands," he announces to the other guys.

"Yeah, we know," Jack jokes, hitching a thumb over towards Seven-legs.

"No, we have an even bigger problem on our hands," Jude parries.

"What?" Theo wonders.

"She's a *human*," Jude spits, pointing at me.

He says the words like it's a curse, and I feel it in my soul that being human and knowing about humans that shift in animals is *not* a good thing. I would be a jumbled mess of even more nerves, except Jude walks up to me, stepping into my personal space.

I'm sooooo not cool with him being in it, at the moment.

Until the man starts taking off his clothes.

With a fluidity that makes me wonder if the Brit is a stripper, Jude deftly pulls off his shirt and jeans. I *literally* feel my jaw drop when he yanks down his boxers, next. Arthur, Theo, and Jack don't even seem fazed by what the crazy man is doing.

I'm pretty sure that my tongue is hanging out—and I'm drooling. I sink into a chair behind me because my knees are weak. To be fair, my resolve to abstain from sex might be far weaker, but Jude is definitely testing me.

When I'm around these men, my world flips upside-down—I suppose I could use some dick to make it feel better. I slide from the chair and sink to the floor on my knees, his dick mouth-wateringly close to my mouth. I stick my tongue and take a quick lick.

Jude yanks away and stumbles back, staring at me in astonishment—I stare right back.

Why take out your cock if you don't want me to suck it?

He answers me nonverbally—*by turning into a fucking insect.*

I've done a lot of dirty shit in my day—*but bestiality isn't one I've ever partaken in.*

Chapter 23

Belle

S *lap.*

        Slap.

Slap.

Something cold and clammy keeps smacking my cheek.

Damn it—*did I get drunk and pass out at a sorority party, again?*

When I crack open an eye, I see that it's just Arthur. He looks paler than normal.

"Hey, love. Are you ok? You went arse over tit there."

"My tits are fine," I mumble, feeling groggy. "What happened?"

Arthur starts to answer before I notice Jude some distance away, standing in the shadows. Everything comes slamming back to me. At least the guy's human and clothed.

Wait—scratch that—this would be way better if he were still naked.

It's the only consolation to the fact that he turns into a bug—*the fact that I got to see his dick in the process.*

Suddenly, I think back to all of our other times together —to our first meeting when I thought it was just a roast.

"Oh, my God! You guys are Animorphs?"

"Shifters," Jack corrects, mussing his grayish-brown hair with his long fingers. "What did you expect? This *is* shifter's anonymous."

I throw up my hands as I sit up quickly. Theo is at my back and places a bracing hand against me for support. I scoot away from him.

"I thought this was sexaholics anonymous!" I defend.

Jude lets out a strangled choke; Arthur and Theo wear identical looks of shock, but Jack—Jack just tips back his head and laughs.

"Love, I don't think you're trying that hard not to be an addict."

I scowl.

"Don't you judge me because I let you touch my asshole up in the bell tower!"

Jude starts to choke even more.

"Dude, swallow," I tell him as he regains his composure and glares at me. "Also, that's what he said."

No one laughs at my joke.

If possible, Jude frowns even more.

"You're in a lot of trouble *and* a lot of danger," he snaps.

"Well, no shit, Sherlock—I've got problems out the wazoo!"

They all stare at me blankly, and I realize this has been our problem all along—these fucking idioms have screwed me over—pun intended.

Instead of joining Sexaholics Anonymous, I've, apparently, joined *Shifter's* Anonymous. I can barely even compute that in my brain. Shifters—actual honest-to-God people who turn into animals—exist, and they have a help group.

"Quick!" I say, throwing my hands. "What came first—the chicken or the egg?"

Arthur stares in confusion, "I. . . I don't know. The chicken?"

"But a chicken has to come from an egg," I argue.

"What does this have to do with anything?" Theo wonders.

"Are you guys humans or animals?" I rephrase the question. "Or are you animals who are humans?"

Jude strokes his chin.

"That's an interesting query. I've never thought about it from that perspective. I'd say that we're humans that can become animals because we're not completely mindless," he finally decides.

"Dude, whatever you need to tell yourself to sleep at night," I joke. "The bigger question is how could you guys have gone this long without figuring it out?!"

Jude gives me a piercing look.

"How could *you* have gone this long without figuring it out?"

Jack speaks up.

"Cut her some slack. She's. . . not that observant."

I glower darkly at him.

"What's that supposed to mean?!" I demand.

Like I'm stupid or something.

Theo winces at me.

"I sent you a picture of my fish. . ." he trails off—like that was an obvious connection to him turning INTO A FUCKING FISH.

I give the blond man a look right back.

"And I sent you a picture of *my vag*."

This seems to get everyone else's attention. Jude, Jack, and Arthur stare at Theo.

"She asked for a picture of my shifter!" he defends. "So, I texted one to her, and she texted me a picture of her cat."

"If by 'cat', you mean 'pussy', then, yes," I snort. "And I asked for a dick pic! Instead, he sent me *this*." I whip out my phone and show them the picture of the fish. "I thought he was being. . . I don't know, *British*."

The four men all look a little affronted at that assessment.

"Well, I just assumed he was being weird. Besides, I sent Theo *this*!"

I show the picture of my shaved Cave of Wonders.

Jack cackles at Theo.

"How could you have thought that was a *cat*?"

"I just thought she was mangled. . . we did think she was a hairless cat!" Theo defends himself.

I choke a bit at these words.

They've thought I was a sphynx cat this entire time?

Dear God, nothing has ever been misinterpreted worse than this whole scenario.

Jude and I palm our faces at the same time.

"Ok, this isn't terrible. I just need to find a *real* Sexaholics Anonymous." Jack coughs at my words. "Screw you, pal! I totally could give up sex! But, given the circumstances, maybe I should just wait six months—I might need some calming down time, ya know?"

He just chuckles.

"That isn't the issue here, love. It's the fact that you know about us and you're *human*."

"Trust me—I want nothing more than to forget about all of this," I reassure him.

"Well, unfortunately, in our world, humans can't know about us," Jude intones.

My spine tingles in apprehension at his dire words.

"And why is that?"

"Because the Tertiaries deigned human knowledge of our existence as a threat. They're afraid that you'll hunt us down like animals, pardon my pun, and will eradicate us."

"I have no intention of doing that!" I refute, before another errant thought pops into my head. "Wait! Are all animals things that can turn into humans?"

"No," Jude responds. "Shifters are very few and far between."

"But how do you know who's a shifter and who's just an animal?"

Jude shrugs.

"Shifters can smell other shifters. There's a difference in the scent. But a human wouldn't know."

I cringe, wondering how many shifters I've accidentally —and maybe purposefully—murdered.

Sorry, mouse shifters, I hate your guts.

"Listen, love," Arthur murmurs, taking my hand. "You're in danger—humans can't know about us. Tertiaries hunt down humans that know about our species."

My hand leaves his palm to fly to my throat.

I know exactly what he means.

He's talking about men who turn into tigers—*and slash women's throats.*

Chapter 24

Theo

THE SLIPPERY DICK

Yep—that's a vagina and I'm a blinkin' prat.

Words cannot describe how gormless[1] I feel for not realizing that Belle sent me a picture of her muff—not to mention how utterly gobsmacked I am that she's human.

Oh, and wanted an actual *dick* pic.

I try hard to focus on the main issue here—Belle's in danger. I listen to Jude, Arthur, and Jack explain shifters to the stunned Yank while attempting not to make any eye contact.

It's bad enough I'm a bloody slippery dick, but this cock-up is on whole other level of brainless. I surreptitiously look at the picture Belle sent again—not because I'm a perv, but because I can't get over my own blindness.

A cat?

I seriously thought *that* was *a cat?*

How long has it been since I've got my end away[2] to make this big of a mistake?

119

"Theo!" Jude shouts, and I startle.

Quickly swiping out of my picture gallery, I darken my phone and look at Jude, finally making eye-contact.

"Sorry—what did you say?"

He's wearing a fierce scowl.

"Belle wants to help," he repeats.

I blink in more confusion.

"Help?" I parrot.

Sucking in a breath of encouragement, I turn to look at beautiful woman. Inwardly, I cringe, prepared for her disgust with me. But, when our eyes connect, I see no censure—just the gentle acceptance that she has always given me.

"She thinks she can help us," Jude elaborates.

"Against the Tershes?" I blurt.

The woman has a death wish.

Jude and Arthur begin lecturing Belle together, but Jack just sits back with an evil grin.

"They aren't going to convince her to leave," he whispers. "Even if it's what's best for her."

Now, I frown.

Does she not understand the peril she is in?!

"I can't believe she managed to fool us all—*unwittingly*!" Jack hoots.

"Yep, and make a fool of me, unwittingly," I chunter[3].

Jack stops laughing to angle himself closer to me.

"Nope—you're not going to do that," he commands.

"Do what?" I ask, mystified.

"Beat yourself up over a mistake," Jack retorts.

I scoff at his words.

"*Mistake?* That's putting it lightly."

"Ah, lighten up, mate—you thought she was sending you a picture of a sphynx cat, not her minge. I mean—don't get me wrong—it's hilarious that you didn't know, but it's not a big deal. We've got bigger problems—not to mention, Belle literally could care less about this mix-up with the pictures. Hell, she's probably more upset you sent her a pic of your fish and not your actual dick," he chortles.

A small grin works its way on my face at Jack's words.

He's right—*Belle probably was pretty miffed about me not sending her a shot of my knob.*

"What are you two whispering about over there?" Arthur wonders.

"Eh, Theo's embarrassed about the picture fiasco," the git admits. "I was just saying that Belle probably is more upset that she didn't receive the pic she wanted more so than she is that Theo thought she was a cat."

Belle flashes a brilliant smile at me.

"Weeeeeeell," she drawls, "it's never to late to send me that dick pic."

I look to the others to see if she's joking—I don't think she is. . .

"Excuse me," I say, standing up.

"Not now, for God's sake!" Jude snaps in exasperation, and Belle pouts.

"What's wrong with now? It's probably the only thing that could make this shit situation better. Actually, I take that back—dick pics from *all of you* would make this better."

Arthur coughs and tugs at his collar.

"Belle, love, there's things about us—and our kind—that you don't understand—" he begins, but our Yank cuts him off.

"Me staying is non-negotiable. A dick pic would just make it better, is all. If I'm going to be killed by a bunch of assholes who turn into big bad wolves, or whatever, I might as well get as many orgasms as I can—and nothing makes me come faster than some naughty photos. And since we're talking dirty—really church these dick pics up for me, please. Hold your cocks hard at the base and squeeze your cranks until they're veiny and throbbing. That really does it for me."

Now, I cough.

Who is this woman—and where has she been all my life?

Chapter 25

Belle

"So, you're a roach," I address Jude, trying to keep the disgust from my voice. "Big deal."

Everyone's face is still slack from my earlier words, and I figure that I'm coming on too strong. I need to back pedal before I make an even bigger ass of myself.

Jude's brow furrows.

"I'm not a cockroach, I'm a cock*chafer*," he corrects.

I shrug.

"What's the difference? They're both bugs."

His scowl deepens.

"No, they're both types of beetles, but cockroaches are from the order *blattodea*, and cockchafers are from the order *coleoptera*. It's like saying that you're a pedophile instead of a nymphophile—they're both interested in sex, but there's a pretty big difference between who they're interested in having sex with."

I stop arguing even though I still think bugs are bugs. Besides, he lost me at 'order'. I hear that word and just think 'food'—*which proves I'm not completely obsessed with sex.*

A sigh escapes me. This disgustingly good looking man, that I've been wanting to fuck since the moment I laid eyes on him, turns into a creepy crawler. It really doesn't matter what kind because a creepy crawler is a creepy crawler.

Oh, I suppose it could be worse—Jude could be one of those bugs that has thousands of legs.

"Well, I'm not going anywhere," I state firmly. "I don't care if you turn into a specific type of beetle, and I don't care if you're a fish and you're a bullfrog."

"Toad—I'm a toad," Arthur also corrects. "There's a difference between toads and frogs."

"Whatever. And if you are a—what are you?" I ask Jack.

"I'm a donkey," he answers.

"Yes, that's right. No wonder you have such a fine ass," I add with a wink. "You guys accept me for the sex freak that I am, and I accept you for the—"

I stop.

Calling them 'animal freaks' might offend them.

"I accept you for how you are," I state firmly, "and I'm not running away. We're going to get through this together."

Jude looks at me like I'm insane.

"There's nothing for you to get through with us. They'll just kill you. Do you not understand this?" he demands.

"I understand," I parry smoothly.

Arthur looks over at Jude.

"I don't think she understands," he whispers.

I throw my hands up in the air.

"What is there to understand? If these Tertiaries get me, I'm dead, correct?"

Jude and Arthur nod.

"I guess she does get it," Jude muses.

Arthur mutters, "Maybe she *is* barmy[1]."

I give him a scathing look.

124

"I'm not insane!" I snap—assuming that's what he means. "I'm just not going to leave you alone because they're going to get you, too."

Jack shrugs

"Maybe. Maybe not. They might think that we were involved in watching them, but they know that there's nothing we can do. There's nothing we would want to do anyways—there's no enforcement in our world. And if there were, they'd be the Tertiaries—the very people who have perpetrated this crime. Primaries are so minuscule to them that they probably won't even bother us. We're like flies."

I frown.

I hate –that to the Tertiaries—the boys are nothing but pests. What a bunch of alpha assholes. I might cut a bitch and make me a fur coat.

"But," Jack presses on, "you, on the other hand, you are not one of us. You're a *human* who knows about us. You are a threat to our well-kept secret—something that the Tertiaries will not stand for. You need to leave this country—immediately."

"In fact, you probably just need to disappear completely." Jude reiterates after Jack is done. "How are we going to do this?"

He starts pacing around worried.

"No, no, no, no. I'm not doing it. We are in this together." I restate sternly. "And I have nowhere to disappear to. Besides, I'm not going to go back to my home. What happens if they do follow me? What happens if they do track me down? Then I'm putting my parents in danger. I'm not doing that. I'd rather be dead than put them in danger."

Jude's shoulder slump. He knows I got him there.

"I'm not going to do anything that would put my family at risk. You're stuck with me." I iterate. "So, what's the plan?

We need to figure out why these guys are trying to break into my apartment and why they killed that woman." Jude frowns.

"We know why they broke into your flat—because they know you're human."

"Ok, then, we need to figure out why they killed that human woman."

Theo raises a brow.

"Did you ever think it's because she found out about shifters?" he queries dryly,

I cringe—I hadn't thought about that.

"Good point. But how random would that be?" I wonder.

"Shifters are pretty secretive," Jack says. "The likelihood of a human finding out about us is pretty well unlikely."

"Exactly," I say. "There's a reason why she got killed. I'm telling you—it's *not* because she knew about shifters. It's something else."

And I plan on figuring it out.

Chapter 26

Belle

"I have an idea," I announce brightly before anyone can keep arguing about why I should not be here. "Let's wake the seven-legged asshole and ask him questions. We don't need a sleuth anywhere. I think we have our answers right here."

The others look at me like I'm insan*er*.

"That's a terrible idea," Arthur disagrees. "If we wake him he can shift."

Arguably, that's a good point because I sure as shit don't ever want him to turn back into that tarantula again.

"Well, I'm not worried about it," I respond airily.

Jack raises his eyebrows.

"Really? Why not?"

"Because I brought my kitchen knives with me just in case," I elucidate.

Jude's eyes widened at my declaration.

Like I'm a homicidal maniac or something.

Perhaps, but I'd rather be that and be prepared than die by tarantula venom.

"If he shifts, we cut off the rest of his legs. If he stays human and tries to run away—we'll cut off his legs," I say cheerfully.

Theo inches his chair back away from me a bit.

I give him a wink to let him know that I'm kind of—not really—teasing.

When nobody moves to make a decision, I walk over to the sleeping shifter and kick him hard in the side. He groans —as do the four men behind me.

"Wake up, asshole. We have questions."

I quickly go over to my backpack that I brought full of knives and other things. Unfortunately, it's not the flamethrower—but I'm getting one of those after this. I take out two knives and pass the backpack to Jude.

"Everyone take a knife," I command.

All the guys do as I've directed, and we wait while Spidey fully comes awake.

"See here, asshole, you shift and I'm cutting off the other seven of your legs. You try to pull anything, and I'll just cut off your human legs. It'll just take me longer."

Hmm, Jude might have been right—I might be homicidal and crazy.

The tarantula shifter's eyes widen at my words. Even though he's duct taped together, he still tries to scuttle away from me like I'm the one he should be afraid of. He should be—I have sharp weapons.

"You!" I say, stabbing a knife in his direction to point. "*You* ruined all my sexual fantasies." His eyes grow even larger. He probably wasn't expecting me to say that. "Instead of sucking his cock," I say, hitching a thumb over at Jude. "He turned into a bug. I mean—never mind what I said!" I quickly cover.

I don't know if I should be telling this guy about Jude.

Does he already know what Jude is?

Does he eat bugs?

I mean, that's what spiders do, right?

Well, only in their shifter form, I assume.

Man, I'm so bad at this whole human to animal thing; I don't know what's going on.

So, I just start swinging the knife around.

That'll make me look a little bit more scary, right?

"Now, we want answers. Why were you trying to break into my apartment?" I snap. He doesn't say anything. "I asked you a question," I hiss, getting closer, but not too close.

I raise the butcher knife higher in the air in warning.

The guy starts mumbling something.

"I don't know what you're saying," I frown before realizing it's because his mouth is duct taped shut.

Inching my way over to him slowly and very carefully with a knife ready, I rip the covering off his mouth. Spidey screams—probably because he has a face full of hair and most of it just came off on the tape. Man, U.K.'s duct tape is really heavy duty. I'm going to send some back to the U.S.

"What was that you were saying," I command imperiously. "And don't lie." I add threateningly. "I have no qualms about cutting up humans as much as I do tarantulas."

That's not true.

I've never hurt a human before in my entire life, I swear.

But he doesn't have to know that, right?

"I'm supposed to bring you into my boss, *Belle Harper*," he sneers.

I twitch when he uses my name.

Great, the fuckers *knows* me.

I swallow heavily and still act like I'm in charge.

"And *what* does your boss want with me?"

The guy shrugs—or tries to, but fails because he's completely bound.

"How am I supposed to know? I'm just working for him."

"Bullshit!" I screech in a slightly unhinged manner, coming closer to him, brandishing my knife.

Spidey lets out a squawk and tries to shimmy back from me, and I smile vengefully.

I feel like Batty from Fern Gully.

I have but one claw—but beware.

In this case, I have but many kitchen knives, but beware.

"Well," I prompt, "you must have some inkling of what he wants."

"He's looking for human women," the shifter finally confesses.

"Human women, for what?" Arthur wonders.

From behind me, the seven-legged freak glares at Arthur.

"I'm not talking to you, scum."

Before I can think of my reaction, I kick the shifter bound in tape—again.

"Don't talk to him that way!" I growl. "He's not less than you because he's some slimy little frog!"

"Toad," Arthur corrects. "I'm a *horny toad.*"

"Er, right. Sorry. He's not less than you because he's a pheromone riddled toad!" I shout.

"No, no, I'm 'horny' because of the bumps on my—" Arthur attempts, but Jack shushes him.

Which is probably a good thing because I'm on a roll.

"Answer the question!" I snap for what feels like the hundredth time. "Why is your boss looking for human women?"

For a dude bound in duct tape, he manages to give me a

sinister as fuck smile. Suddenly, I feel like the tables have been turned.

A feeling of premonition creeps over me when he says, "To experiment on."

Motherfucker.

I definitely need a flamethrower.

Chapter 27

Jude
THE COCKCHAFER

Tertiary are experimenting on humans?

My mind races as I try to find an explanation as to why, and I can see that Arthur, Theo and Jack are doing the same thing. I turn to the Tertiary to ask him why—*but I'm not given the chance.*

Against his better judgment, the Tersh shifted into his tarantula form.

Belle lets out an ear-piercing scream. The foolish man cannot move as the fine hairs of his body are caught up in the duct tape. He looks like a spider football. Belle *still* hasn't quit screaming and she runs over and kicks it—ironically—*like it's a football.*

It bounces against the wall and comes launching back towards her. She jumps out of the way, and it comes towards me. Without thinking, I do the same thing that she did and kick. It goes to Jack—who kicks to Arthur.

Who kicks it to Leo.

Who kicks it back towards Belle.

Who throws a knife at it.

The blade hits the tarantula dead center, piercing it from one end to the other—I don't know if this is purely by luck, or she's just that skilled—either way, I don't ever plan to piss her off.

The Tertiary starts twitching before slowly ceasing to move. Its body instantly stiffens into rigor mortis and starts blackening, as if mold is creeping upon it.

"What's happening?" Belle whispers, her face deathly pale.

"This is what happens to shifters when we die— rigor mortis sets in immediately, and then, a petrification process begins. Shortly afterwards, the body hardens to the point of rock. Then, it's like ashes, and it crumbles away. There's never any trace left of the shifter. This is why my species has survived so long— because shifters do not leave behind any trace of them," I explain gently.

Belle is shaking again.

"Oh, God. Oh, God. I've killed him. I'm a murder. Do I go to jail for this? Did I kill a human? Does it not count when he's like this? Oh, God. What about if they were an endangered species?"

"It's ok, love. I think we have bigger problems on our hands. You're obviously in danger. We don't know who his boss is, and we don't know what they want with humans— aside from *experimenting on them*," I emphasize those last words so that she understands this could be worse than death.

I have no idea why Tertiaries would want someone like Belle; or even what they want with humans, in general. I certainly know that they find them expendable, though. Humans to Tershes are like flies to humans. They have no problem killing them—or worse—experimenting and torturing them because they find them inferior.

"Belle, I know you don't want to bring danger to your family, but the best thing that you can do right now is *leave*. You need to get out of this country. Go back to yours. From there, we can formulate a plan, but at least put an ocean between you and us," I plead.

It's very easy for Tertiaries to spread word—there are so many of them that can live by land, sea, or air—but I don't bother telling her this.

I don't want to scare her more.

But I do think that her being here is a dangerous decision—*and an unwise one*.

Tertiaries, as a whole, look down on Secondaries and Primaries but, within their ranks, they don't necessarily work together—especially if they're solitary apex hunters, like the tiger that Belle saw kill the woman.

If this is who the tarantula shifter's boss was, it's very unlikely that this unknown man is in touch with other apex Tertiaries. Therefore, he will probably want to hunt Belle himself, but it would probably be an inconvenience if she's an ocean away—and not worth the bother.

Even so, Belle will need to constantly be on the move and most likely have to change her identity.

I frown.

Where would she even begin to do this?

Suddenly, I remember that Sian has a cousin who's into sheisty shit—maybe he can help her. I quickly send a text message to Sian to meet me at the apartment—we need to start packing our Yank's bags immediately.

"Belle, love, we've got to go now," I reiterate.

She's still staring at the Tertiary who's already crumbled into dust—the church's cleaning person will think of nothing more than somebody likely dumped a pile of ashes into the center of the floor.

"Is this what happens to you all when you die?" Belle asks me with tears in her eyes.

"Yep, basically a free cremation," Jack jokes.

I give them a look.

"Now's not the time," I hiss.

Jack just shrugs. He's of the mind that if you don't laugh, you cry—and, clearly, Belle is on the brink of tears.

"Come on, love. We're going to get you back to your flat. You need to go into the university's main office first thing in the morning and tell them that you won't be able to study here anymore."

Belle's lip quivers at my announcement.

Poor Mite has been through so much—now, to tell her that she won't be able to even get her degree anymore must be devastating, but I'm sure there are plenty of American universities she can go to.

Although, I personally wouldn't recommend it.

Belle's going to want to stay under the radar the rest of her life—if she wants to keep living and not be caught by the man who wants to experiment on her.

I take her hand and squeeze.

"It's going to be all right," I swear.

Belle looks over at me and manages to crack a grin.

"And to think none of this would have happened if I had just kept on being a sexaholic," she teases.

I sweep her into a fierce hug and kiss the top of her colorful head.

I hate the danger our little Yank is in, but I thank God every day that she, somehow, stumbled into our lives.

And I'll do anything to protect this sweet summer child— even at the cost of my own life.

Chapter 28

Belle

Humans can turn into animals—who would've thunk?

Certainly *not* me.

I'm just a sex addict who was looking to get cured.

Instead, I stumbled upon a deadly secret, and I *still* want to fuck everyone.

The car ride back to Oxford is silent as we head south toward the university. Inside, I'm packed in with Jack and Arthur again—Theo and Jude took Jude's car. The very air within the speeding vehicle feels charged with tension.

Clearly, I have a target on my back.

I just hope that Jude is right, and once I get back to the States, everything will go back to normal. I mean, what happens if this boss-man does send people—animals. . . *whatever*—over the ocean after me?

What then?!

What happens if they send a bee to track me?

I'm allergic to bees—I'll die if the little bastard stings me!

Or what happens if Shifter Boss sends an octopus, and it

strangles me to death with its eight arms while I'm in the bathtub?!

Great.

Now I'm afraid of bathing and octopuses—and here I thought they were awesome because the males could take off their dicks and throw them at the women.

Wouldn't that be great?!

It would just be raining dick, dick, dick, dick, dick, but it's not raining dick in my world—it's raining shit scenarios.

This is worse than when my folks told me about the birds and the bees—that was just awkward. Now, I'm legit afraid of birds and bees. Who knows which ones are humans in disguise. And who knows which ones might be after me!

Probably the most disappointing thing of all is that I'm not going to walk out of here with my scholarship.

Ok, maybe it's the fact that I didn't get to bang Jude, Theo, Sian, and Elise—let's just agree there's a lot of disappointment going around.

Being an Oxford grad was going to be big for me, though. And, as much as I tell myself that the university was going to take away my scholarship from me because of my slutty sexcapades, I don't know that for a fact. I could have rode out my skankiness for another two years and left here with a degree *and* being the first person to sleep with the entire student body.

Hashtag life goals.

Well, maybe I'll be able to do some online courses under a fake name when I get home. . . it just seems like such a waste.

Of course, my life is more important—but there's no guarantee that once they get home that I'll be safe!

I don't say any of this out loud, Jack and Arthur look like

they have enough to worry about—not to mention Theo. That man needs his eyes checked.

If you can't tell a Sphinx cat from a well-shaved vagina— you're not getting laid enough.

When we get back to campus, we book it to my apartment building, passing campus security. Apparently, they're searching around for a runaway donkey. . . this makes Jack laugh uproariously. I half-wave at the two guards—who just give me a look.

They're probably wondering if I'm going to tie up the new men with me.

Did I mention that Jack and Arthur are still in various states of disarray?

The pissy security guard frowns at me as we hustle by, but I have bigger fish to fry than pleasing that guy. Jack and Arthur enter into my room first to search it—but it really doesn't do anything to ease my fear.

What if there's a maggot shifter or some other small-assed animal hiding in there waiting to pounce on me in all his buggy nastiness?

I'll squash his ass—that's what I'll do. I have no qualms about killing those fuckers. . . except, Jude's a bug, too. I would never squish him, though, even if I hate bugs.

Because I like Jude.

And I love his dick.

I shake my head.

It's not nice not to kill someone because you like their dick, right?

Ugh.

I swear this whole situation has made me mental!

Thank God shifters can't read minds because my thoughts are questionable.

Besides, I have to trust that Jack and Arthur can smell if

any other shifters are inside—which they don't. I enter hesitantly before going to work packing all my shit haphazardly in my suitcases.

Suddenly, there's a knock at the door. Arthur peeks through before opening it to allow Elise and Sian to walk through.

"Jude told us everything," Sian sniffles.

"You poor dear!" Elise moans. "How could we have been so blind? We kept mistaking you for a cat, but you just like pussy—something Sian and I totally should have picked up on!"

I take her hands into mine and squeeze.

"It's ok—I was just as blind."

Sian looks sad.

"Oh, we could have had a threesome," she bemoans.

Now, I want to cry—knowing this secret has ruined a lesbian threesome for me! Now, I'll never get to cross that off my bucket list...

Again.

"Can we at least snuggle together, and I accidentally cop a feel under your shirts before I leave?" I ask hopefully.

Sian giggles and sits down on my couch.

"Come here, love. We can cuddle until the offices open. You deserve it."

I rush over before she retracts her offer but, oddly enough, I don't make a move. I'm content to just lay in her arms and let her hold me, while Elise runs a soft hand over my hair.

I feel safe and loved.

Jude and Theo eventually return. No one says a word, but all the guys join us at the foot of the couch, placing a hand somewhere on my body.

We're all connected with me at the center—it's the most incredible feeling ever.

I fall asleep with a smile on my face.

Who would have thunk Belle Harper could have a sleep over without it turning into an orgy?

Chapter 29

Belle

"Good morning, Mrs. Wanker!"

"It's Wonker," the crochety secretary from the counselor's office corrects.

"My B," I non-apologize. "Can I see Mr. Fields?"

Mrs. Wonker purses her lips in a thin line and glares at me—she's not a particular fan of mine. I might have seduced way too many people in her office and never tried to seduce her.

She's bitter, not better.

"Can I please speak with my counselor?"

"Mr. Fields is out of the office."

"Well, it's an emergency," I insist, smoothing my gorgeous rainbow pastel maxi skirt.

I've paired it with a white tank and some cute sandals. I look bangin'—*peeps better watch out.*

"Unfortunately, Ms. Harper, they're gone until term starts."

"I'm not going to be here for term," I mumble.

Mrs. Wonker perks up.

"Why not?" she demands, hungry for gossip.

"It's personal," I snap in a hoity-toity tone.

"You're up the duff, aren't you?!" the secretary cackles with glee.

I look around confused.

"What duff?"

"It means you're pregnant," she explains with an eye roll.

I instinctively place a hand on my flat stomach.

"I doubt it—I swallow all my kids."

Mrs. Wonker blanches.

"How incredibly crass, Ms. Harper."

"Whelp, being crass is what gets me ass," I sing. "So, back to my emergency—is there a counselor I can speak to? I really need to get back home."

She looks me over again.

"You do terrible things," the old witch judges, "but let me go see what I can do."

She fluffs her hair and walks off into the back, only to return fairly quickly—so quickly, I doubt she actually did much but mentally flip me off.

"I'm sorry, but no one can help you," she tells me with sickly sweet insincerity.

"Listen, Mrs. *Wanker*, I'm getting on a plane to go back home today, so I really would like to do this in person because I have my concerns about the person who handles the calls."

It's a direct insult since *she's* the one who handles the calls.

"Well, it looks like there's nothing I can do," she says tightly. "I guess you better just leave."

Suddenly, the door chimes and in steps Dean Hardwick.

"Miss Harper!" he chirps. The unease I felt from before

grows tenfold now that I'm in his presence. "What are you doing this fine morning?"

"Oh, I was just telling Mrs. Wanker here—I mean, Wonker—that I need to go back home because of a family emergency."

The secretary sniffs.

"You didn't say anything about your family," she complains.

"I said it was personal—which meant it wasn't any of your business—emergency."

She glares.

"I still think you're up the duff," she mutters under her breath.

I give the dean a pointed look.

"This is who you hired? Someone without manners and compassion?"

He gives her a censorious frown.

"I apologize, Miss Harper. We do not speak this way to our students!"

Mrs. Wonker pales at his words and sits back down meekly.

I grin smugly.

"No indeed. Quite *crass* if you ask me," I drawl evilly.

"Come with me, my dear. I will take care of you personally!"

I grimace—I'd rather stay with Lady Wanker.

"Come, we will get your friends, and we'll go talk. I will help you however I can."

My eyes widen at his words—*my friends*?

What the hell is Dean Stiffdick insinuating?

I knew something was off about this guy.

Anyone over the age of puberty not interested in me sexually is truly suspect.

The creep is totally an animorph—and he knows about my best friends—my non sexaholics. I give Dean Fuckface a tight smile.

"Great," I respond. "Thanks for your help, Mrs. Wanker."

She doesn't bother correcting me.

The dean leads me out of the office into another building where his is. I'm like a sweet innocent sheep following the wolf into his lair.

Well, I'm not that innocent—sexually speaking—but I might be the dumbest person on earth for not running. In truth, I'm terrified that this man has done something to my friends, and I might be the only one who can save them.

"Miss Harper, I've been looking into you," the dean says genially as we walk.

"Really? You don't say," I reply as blandly as possible.

"You have one of our most prestigious scholarships here at the university," he continues. "It would be such a shame for you to have to cancel that. After you address your family emergency and return, the scholarship will still be waiting for you. But, having said that, we have a, ah, certain standard that we must keep up here at Oxford. Namely, one that you don't associate yourself with those *lesser* than you."

"You mean like the prostitutes I sometimes hire?" I blurt out.

The guy doesn't even blink.

"I'm talking about the group of misfit Primaries that you befriended... I know that you know about us," he whispers.

Awesome.

The dean knows that I know about his kind.

But, on the upside, he doesn't seem to have a problem that I'm an absolute whore.

"Your little friends are simply not fit for society—let alone for Oxford standards."

I make a face.

I admit that I'm going to school here because I want a good education, but trust me when I say they're snobby as all get out. It totally grinds my gears.

"So, you and I will come to an agreement about your friends. . . or else I'll make them disappear," he finishes silkily.

We've finally reached his office door, and Dean Hardwick pushes it open.

"Would you like to see them?" he invites.

I step inside, horrified at what this bastard has done to my friends—but the room is empty.

There's no Jude, Jack, Arthur, Theo, Elise, or Sian.

There's no one. . .

Except him and me.

The dean swiftly closes the door and locks it behind him before I realize that the fucker has played me—and I walked neatly into his trap.

Because I'm an idiot, and now, I'm about to die.

Chapter 30

Arthur

THE HORNY TOAD

"Please, stop sniffing my arse!" Jack growls at Theo.

All morning, Jude, Jack, Theo, and I have been patrolling campus. Thankfully, we haven't smelled any shifters on the grounds, but Theo is getting on Jack's last nerve. Poor bloke is terrified and sticking close to the donkey shifter.

This is the third time he's bumped into Jack.

"Let's head back to Belle's flat," I suggest before my best ass strangles my best fish.

We need to haul arse back and get her ready to leave the country immediately—*and then, the lot of us need to get lost for a while.*

When I approach the door to Belle's room, I hear soft feminine murmurs on the other side. I walk in, but only Sian and Elise are there.

"Where's Belle?" I bark.

"She went to the office to tell them that she won't be here this semester," Elise responds.

"She wasn't supposed to go anywhere alone!" I snap.

Elise rolls her eyes.

"She went in broad daylight with plenty of other people milling around. Besides, she didn't want us to go with her. I think she's upset and needs her space," she says.

I throw up my hands in exasperation.

Sian stares at me with glassy eyes that are unnerving.

"We both know she's not going to make it," she whispers.

My jaw drops open.

"Quit speaking about her like she has a terminal illness!" I growl.

"That's not it and you know it!" Elise defends her girlfriend.

"It doesn't matter where we move her," Sian continues, deaf to Elise and me. "Her smell will always be trackable—she'll always be traceable. She's too much of a threat. They're never going to let this go. Even if she goes back to America."

She moans the last words as if in genuine pain, and my stomach twists sickeningly at her words.

I know that she's right—I know that Belle is a dead woman walking.

I just keep praying and hoping that if we get her on a plane, she'll be too much of a hassle to deal with, even if she's trackable. The truth is that sending her home isn't good enough—she needs to completely and utterly disappear.

Basically, Belle requires a whole new identity, a whole new life, *a whole new scent to be non-traceable.* I know Jude spoke to Sian's cousin who is shifter shady, but can he really pull off what Belle needs to completely blend into the woodwork?

Doubtful.

I don't know anyone or anything that can erase someone's scent.

Jack comes charging into the room.

"What's wrong, Sian? Is it Belle? Is she all right?" he asks frantically.

The titmouse shifter sniffles.

"She's fine, Jack. I'm just. . . gutted. You know that Belle will never be safe."

Jack locks eyes with me and runs an impatient hand through his grayish-brown hair—he always does this when he's agitated.

"We'll find a way!" he vows more to himself than to Sian. "I won't let *anything* happen to her."

Elise tips her head at the vehemence in Jack's voice—I hear it, too.

Is Jack falling in love with the gorgeous conundrum that dropped into our laps?

I'm not left to ponder this—nor why the thought tightens my chest—because Jack stomps through the flat, calling for Belle.

"She's not here," Elise explains once more.

"WHERE IS SHE?!" Jack demands in a fiercer voice than mine.

"Ugh!" the booby shifter sighs in disgust. "She went to the office—stop having a paddy[1]! She'll be right back."

Jack rounds on me.

"Belle's alone?!"

"That's what I said!" I say with vindication.

"What's going on?" Jude wonders as he enters with Theo.

"Elise and Sian let Belle jot across campus—*alone!*" Jack sneers.

"Enough!" Elise snaps. "Stop acting like you're the only one here with feelings invested in Belle! We all care about her—or are you too blind to notice? Sian and I didn't act out of ignorance or because we're too wrapped up in ourselves. Belle needed some alone time—plain and simple. I understand what's at stake, but she's going across campus in broad daylight. Belle, also, understands the danger she's in. If you're so concerned, go after her, but I think she deserves fifteen minutes of time to decompress."

Jude thoughtfully strokes his chin.

"The girls are right," he finally decrees.

Jack mutters something angrily under his breath, but Jude just raises a hand for silence.

"I will shift and go fly overhead to keep an eye on her. Belle needs some space, but that doesn't mean she's safe. I will keep an eye on her—at a distance—so everyone gets what they want."

He quickly strips and shifts before anyone can argue with him. Jude buzzes near the window, and I leap over to open it for him to fly out.

There's a moment of awkward silence before Jack addresses the birds.

"I'm sorry," he apologizes.

Sian nods her acceptance, but Elise just sniffs in affront.

"Come on, Leez," he begs the booby. "I'm just. . . worried—"

"And we're not?!" she snarks.

"I didn't say that!" Jack retorts in defense. "I care for Belle—I mean, I have a different connection with her, I think—"

"She screwed Arthur, too, so I doubt it," Elise responds icily.

Jack looks at me sheepishly.

"I think we all care about her. . . *deeply*," I offer.

The ass shifter stares at me intently before acknowledging my words.

"Then, I guess we'll all do whatever it takes to keep her safe."

There's a hum of agreement and, once more, we're working together as a team with a common goal.

Suddenly, Jude flits back through the window and shifts mid-air. He lands gracefully on his feet, but his eyes are panicky.

"Belle's gone! I can't scent her anywhere on campus— nor can I find her!" Jude's frantic tone puts us all in a state of agitation—he's always the calm during the storm. "I can just vaguely smell her near one building, come on!"

Jude hastily pulls on some clothes, and we race across campus. Just as he said, I can faintly smell traces of Belle on the front steps of the office building, but there's no indication of which direction she went—it's like she just *vanished*.

"How are we going to find her?" Sian cries.

"We need a tracker," Theo concludes.

My innards protest at the thought of Belle missing—our time to save her at this point is dwindling.

There is little chance we'll be able to get to her in time before the Tertiaries kill her—*if they haven't already*.

"I know someone!" Jack yells. "Best tracker around—and he owes me big time."

"Great—call him now!" Jude orders, but Jack is already dialing the number.

For our sake, I hope this tracker is a miracle worker—because we're going to need one.

Chapter 31

Belle

"Wake up, Miss Harper. We have things to do," a familiar voice commands me in my ear.

My eyes slit open, and I find myself bound in an unrecognizable area. From what I can see, it looks like a cemented area with fluorescent lights and cages.

That's right—*cages.*

It's exactly like something I would expect to find if somebody ran an underground cockfighting ring. I look back over at the man who woke me up and see Dean Hardwick.

"Are you a tarantula?" I blurt out.

The dean tips back his head and laughs.

"No, no, my dear, I'm even higher on the food chain."

I cringe—that doesn't sound good at all.

"I think there's been some mistake. I don't want to know about you, and I'm not going to tell anyone—" I start to reassure before shutting my mouth.

Spidey's last words pop into my brain and cut me off—his boss was looking for human women *to experiment on. . .*

Whelp, fuck a duck.

Dean Hardwick is the boss, isn't he?

Of course, he is—*because why not?*

This is what I get for thinking like a fourteen year old boy. All the blood has pooled in my phantom cock that I probably will tell Dean Stiffdick to suck before he eats me in a very non-sexy way.

"Maybe you're confused. I'm not the whore you're looking for," I joke.

If a bad *Star Wars* pun doesn't save my skanky ass, nothing will.

"You're exactly what I'm looking for, my dear." the dean disagrees.

Well, that sucks for me.

"I don't think so," I counter. "I bet there's a lot better human women out there for you."

I acknowledge that this isn't the responsible thing to do because I certainly don't want other women to be tested on.

But I also don't want myself to be tested on.

"How about you let me go and we call it good? I'll just hop back over the pond and never step foot in the UK again, deal?"

"Oh, no, no, no, no—that won't do at all! I promise that you're exactly the type of woman I've been looking for—I've heard the rumors about you on campus among the professors. . ." the dean trails off.

"That I'm brilliant?" I attempt.

"No," he chuckles darkly, "that you're a blint—and that's exactly what I'm looking for."

"Blint?"

"*Whore*—you're a whore," he clarifies.

"You know, in my defense, I'm not the only whore at Oxford," I point out. "There's plenty of them—I should know since I've slept with a lot of them, and I can help you find them."

Shut up, Belle!

What am I even saying?

I need to be quiet and just find a way out of this without getting anyone else stuck in the same predicament.

"Well, no, I'm not just looking for any old skank," Dean Hardwick argues. "I'm looking for someone very particular. A one-of-a-kind slut, if you would."

Now, normally, I would take his words as a compliment, but being a 'one-of-a-kind slut' really doesn't sound like that's in my favor right now.

"I promise you that being skanky isn't that unique," I whimper.

"No, it's not—but your blood is," he whispers reverently, and I swear said blood freezes in my veins at his words. "See, shifters can smell very well."

I nod.

Unfortunately, I know all too well now that shifters have a unique sense of smell—a heightened one.

"Especially my type of shifter," the dean adds with a rather wolfish grin. "I'm one of the most feared animals of all time."

"Oh my God—you're a T-Rex?!" I cry.

Then, I freeze.

He can't see me if I don't move, right?

"No, you daft woman, they're extinct!"

"You're a mosquito, then?"

"A mosquito?!" Dean Stiffdick sneers. "Why would anyone be afraid of a mosquito?"

"Haven't you ever read a book?" I scoff. "Some *dean* you are—mosquitos are the deadliest animals on Earth!"

He raises a brow.

"Sometimes, I forget you're hiding a brain behind that pretty face and your whorish mannerisms," he backwards compliments.

"Er... thanks?"

"See, I already knew that you were special," he continues, "but I took a vial of your blood while you were sleeping to confirm it."

I give the fucked-up bastard a look—sleeping is just a quaint way to say that he knocked me out.

"Dude, I don't know about your laws here in the UK, but that's a serious violation of my rights!"

Dean Hardwick smirks.

"You're so cute, Miss Harper. See, your human laws are not something that I have to abide by—in my world, *I am the law.*"

Sheesh, someone has a God complex.

"And because I'm the law," he continues, "I can do whatever I want, whenever I feel like it—and what I want, Jezebel, *is your womb.*"

"Eww, gross! What are you going to do with it?" I cry out.

What kind of pervert is this dude?!

Is he some kind of shifter that craves women's reproductive organs?

Is he like a cannibal, but not?

"I promise it probably wouldn't taste that good," I exclaim, trying to divert his attention.

"My child, you watch way too many *American* movies," he sneers.

"Can I just say that I don't really appreciate the emphasis you just put on American—like we're a bunch of imbeciles," I frown. I would totally defend my country and people more if the situation weren't so dire, but this is a serious shitstorm.

Dean Boner wants my motherfucking sperm hotel!

"Now, see here, you can't just take my womb. What are you going to do—just reach up in there and yank it out?!"

I almost cry at the thought, but the dean rolls his eyes.

"Stop being so melodramatic, Miss Harper. I want nothing of the such. Your womb is no use of me outside your body. I need it inside of you."

"For what?" I ask in confusion.

"For exactly what it's meant to do, my dear," he responds condescendingly.

"Wombs are for housing babies," I point out.

"Exactly, Miss Harper."

And then it dawns on me—*this crazy fuck is going to use me as a breeder.*

Chapter 32

Belle

"I'm on the pill!" I shout loudly, the sound reverberating around the large empty room.

Dean Hardwick waves a hand.

"No worries. It's nothing that my scientists haven't already taken into account."

Great.

The psycho has scientists.

"All we need to do is give you a shot to put you into ovulation."

Body, if you're listening to me, don't go into ovulation. This crazy man is going to hijack our eggs—and womb—and make monster babies out of them. . . in me.

I can see the future now—a world full of slutty little Belles that can turn into God-knows-what-kind of animal.

"What we're going to do is inject you with a special serum created just for women with your blood type. You'll start ovulating, and then, we'll bring in our finest shifters."

"I can reassure you I've actually already had sex with some of your finest shifters," I say.

The dean looks a little confused, and I quickly shut my mouth. I'm probably just getting Arthur and Jack into a lot of trouble. "I mean, bring on these shifter studs."

I want to smack my stupid self—I can't, though, because I'm bound.

"That's the spirit," the dean praises. "I'll be right back."

"OK, self," I pep-talk when he's out of sight. "This is the time where all those hidden powers that you've read about your entire life in book and movie characters needs to manifest. We need to break out of here and get away before they make us their shifter whore."

My mind kind of sidles at that word—as if intrigued by it.

No brain! We are not intrigued about being a shifter whore!

Seriously, my hormones need to get their shit together. This could be life or death—I can't give birth to a shifter, and Dean Hardwick makes it sound like I need to pop out one or more of these puppies.

I mean, I say puppies, but who knows what they'll be!

I wiggle my arms as best as I can, trying to break the rope. As someone who has been tied up a lot and who has tied up a lot of people, I'm actually pretty proficient with knots. Unfortunately, this one must have been done by a Shibari master.

I try for three minutes solid and only chafe my wrists as my reward. Of course, the shifter bad guys return in that time. If my life were a story—I would shut the book. I would be really pissed at the author because this sucks donkey balls.

And, thanks to Jack, I can say I've sucked donkey balls—this is by far way worse.

I would take Jack's ass tea-bagging me *any* day of the week over what's about to happen to me now.

"Listen, fellas," I start when the dean returns with another guy.

I assume that he's the scientist. The man has a balding head and *Harry Potter*-style glasses—basically, just the very typical geeky look that you would assume someone in this position would have.

It's slightly reassuring in the sense that he probably knows what he's doing—but, also, that he knows what he's doing, and I'm going to instantly pop out eggs that they're going to harvest to make creepy ass shifters.

"Darling, you have nothing to barter with," Dean Stiffdick cuts me off. "I'm wealthy beyond my means and the highest of my kind. There's nothing that you have to offer me except what I want from you."

"Not true," I negate. "Not true at all—you haven't had a blowjob from me. And, if you listen to the whispers on campus, you will know how awesome they are. I use both my hands in combination with my mouth, so it's kind of like a two-for-one deal."

I try adding in a wink, but it's hard when you're terrified and trying to bamboozle somebody out of a situation instead of really attempting to seduce them.

"Wow. You weren't kidding," the scientist mutters. "She really is a slut."

"Whoa, whoa, whoa!" I screech. "Uncalled for! You're not going to shame me, sir. If I want to use my fantastic oral skills to get out of speeding tickets, or in shitty situations like this, then bully for me!"

I realize that I'm probably not really helping myself, but I'm throwing everything I have out there. I don't have anything else to offer besides my great oral skills.

"My dear, the only thing I want from you is to be my high-end kerb girl," the dean responds.

"Kerb girl?" I parrot in confusion because—one thing I've learned—*everything* has been lost in translation thus far.

"Prostitute," Dean Hardwick clarifies. "You're going to be my personal prostitute to do with when I say and I how I say."

"Ooooo, *a prostitute*. I didn't realize that I was getting paid for this job," I retort snidely.

"Yes—as long as your womb keeps producing—you'll keep living."

I cringe.

I suppose living is sufficient enough payment.

"I'll go get the others, Dr. Pilkins. Just get her prepped and ready," the dean commands to the scientist.

A shudder racks my body at 'prepped and ready'.

Doctor Asswipe doesn't waste any time to follow the dean's orders. He steps right up, cleans a patch of my skin on my arm, and plunges a needle—*and all its contents*—right into me. I scream as the doc steps back.

"Really, Miss Harper, there's no need for that," the man chides.

He's right—I didn't feel any pain.

I just screamed for the sheer need to be vocal about how I feel inside—*used.*

Dirty.

Violated.

"You can't do this! You don't have my consent!" I scream.

The doctor pats my hand like a comforting uncle.

"Then, I'm afraid it's going to get far worse for you," he reasons coolly as Dr. Shouldn't Have A License undoes the ties over my legs and spreads them open wide. "But, I have a feeling someone like *you* will enjoy what's coming next."

I despise the way he emphasizes 'you'—like because I'm

a sex addict and enjoy getting fucked, it's ok if I don't give my consent. *I'll eventually get into it* is his rationale.

Fuck that and fuck him.

Some people might get their jollies off to that shit—but I do not.

Of course, there's no point in arguing with Dr. Idiot—besides, I have bigger problems. Dean Hardwick just returned. With him are three other men—three *very familiar* men.

Two are from Professor Yardley's office the first time I met the dean. And the third. . . the last time I saw him, he was blending into the shadows.

And slashing a woman's throat out with his tiger paw.

Chapter 33

Jack
THE ASS

"*You ain't nothin' but a hound dog,*" my ring tone sings as I quickly answer my phone.

"Hey, Jepssum. Thanks for calling."

"What's up, Jack? What can I do for you?" the older man asks on the other line.

I look over at the others, inches away, but I know that they'll still be able to hear.

"Listen, remember that favor you owe me?"

"You mean when you came as a donkey to my kid's birthday party for the petting zoo, and everyone tried to pin the tail on your arse?"

I hear a few snorts from Sian and Elise trying to cover their chuckles behind me.

"Yep, that's the one, and I'm calling it in now. I need you to meet me at Oxford University immediately—"

"Slow down, son. I'm not as young as I used to be. I can be there in a few hours, give or take, depending on—"

"It's a matter of life and death, Jep!" I cut off.

There's a bit of silence.

"Matter of life and death, you say?"

"Yes!"

"I'll be there as quickly as I can," he promises before hanging up the phone.

Now, all we can do is wait.

Sian shifts into her titmouse and flies overhead to keep an eye out for my hound dog friend. About fifteen minutes later, she comes back as herself.

"Jep's on his way about a quarter kilometer out," she tells us.

Sure enough, I can hear the barking and the howls as the hound gets closer. Soon, Jep appears, and I go jogging over to him. I scratch behind his ear and his tail wags—but his eyes narrow.

Just because he has an animal reaction doesn't mean that the human inside likes me treating him like a dog.

"Good boy," I tease and chuckle when he swipes a paw at me. "I'm kidding! I'm kidding! It's a good thing that talking to your dog is considered normal. Come with me, I've got something for you."

I bring him over around the building where Belle last was and explain to Jep what happened. His eyes get larger and larger and I know what he's thinking—humans can't know about us.

"Please, Jep—I'm begging you. I know I'm asking a lot from you but, please, help us track her."

The hound dog gives me a hard look, but ultimately gives a sharp nod.

"Thank you," I say gratefully. "Thank you so much." Behind me, I motion Jude, Arthur, Theo, Elise and Sian forward. "Come on, you lot. Let's go find our Yank."

Theo steps up to Jep, pulling something out of his

Shifters Anonymous

pocket.

"This is hers," he says to the shifter, holding it under his nose to sniff.

It's a pair of thong underwear.

I give Theo a look.

"Why do you have a pair of Belle's knickers in your pockets, mate?"

Theo clears his throat awkwardly.

"I forgot she stuffed them in there..."

He trails off sheepishly, flushing when the girls snicker. I just roll my eyes.

Of course, he blames our lovely sex addict, but it's more likely that Belle put them there than Theo stealing the lacy scrap of fabric—he's a timid bloke.

Jep takes another deep inhale before putting his snout to the ground. He gives a brisk bark and starts running off. We all chase after him. The hound makes it to the tree line that borders the property of the university before ducking behind a tree. He comes back out as a man shielding his privates and motions for us to come over.

"Definitely smells like a Tertiary took her through these woods. I can track their scents, but you all are going to have to follow me in a vehicle."

I take a big whiff and wrinkle my nose.

Around me, Jude, Theo, Arthur, Elise, and Sian are doing the same—and I can read their confusion because it mirrors mine.

"What Tertiary?" I ask Jep.

He scratches his head.

"Smells like a wolf, maybe. Something's off, as if someone's tried to mask it, but it's still there."

"Fuck," Jude curses. "No wonder we didn't smell

anything on campus. Those bastards have been here the entire time—Belle's been in danger all along!"

"Stop," I order Jude, knowing exactly where his thoughts are going. "This isn't your fault. It's not my fault—it's not any of our faults. Let's just go and save our girl."

Elise steps forward and takes off her collar necklace that is just a simple ribbon with the choker.

"Here, take this in case we get separated," she tells Jep as he shifts back into a dog.

Sweeping her long dark hair out of her face, she kneels before the hound and rigs the string so that it wraps around her phone and ties around his neck at the same time.

"Call 'Tittie' so we can follow you better or when you find something."

Jep barks once in agreement before disappearing into the woods.

"Come on, everyone! Jude's vehicle is parked over there. We need to get in and circle around," Arthur directs.

We race over and all squeeze in like it's a clown car for shifters. Suddenly, Sian's phone begins to ring.

"What'd you find?" she asks Jep, putting him on speaker.

"The Tershes met a 2015 Volkswagen Amarok here at the edge of the woods. I can't smell your girl's scent anymore, but I can track their truck."

"You can smell the make and model?!" I ask incredulously.

"Right down to the paint color—even that has a unique scent."

I look at Jude, who looks damn impressed.

Hell—I'm damned impressed.

"Which way?" Arthur wants to know.

"They went north on the tarmac[1]. Let me meet you. I can get in and track while riding if you roll down the windows. If I bark three times, that means stop. I'm going to shift now. Tell your pretty friend that I can't retie the necklace, but I'll carry it and her phone back in my mouth."

"Thank you!" Elise says.

"Give me five minutes," Jep huffs before disconnecting.

It takes even less time for him to reappear at the side of the road. Our crowded truck becomes even more so as he climbs into Elise's lap and drops her phone and jewelry beside her.

I roll down the windows and drive north as directed. We don't stop until we're past Banbury by about fifteen minutes. Just when I'm about to ask questions to a dog, Jep barks sharply three times, and Arthur slams on the brakes. The hound dog shifter jumps out of the car window and lands nimbly on his feet before changing back into his human form.

"The truck went this way, and I can smell your girl again. She's down this road—they all are."

"They?" Theo asks with apprehension.

"Tertiaries—five of them. Be careful. This is as far as I'm going."

"Thanks, Jep," I say gratefully, shaking his hand.

"Watch yourself, Jack. This is no place for an ass—nor the others," he warns, waving to my fellow Primaries.

"I know," I murmur.

We're likely walking to our deaths.

"This Yank must be something special," Jep comments.

I smile.

"She's. . ." I trail off, at a loss of how to describe Belle.

"She's one-of-a-kind," Jude fills in for me.

The rest of us all nod in agreement.

"Good luck finding your unicorn, then," Jep says with heartfelt sincerity before shifting and running back south.

"Girls—shift and go back to Sian's cousin's place. We'll keep our phones in the car and tell you when we get back to campus. We'll go get Belle," I promise. "Come on, lads, lets shift and check this out."

We all strip and change into our animals, except Theo. Together, we make our way silently down the path. After a half a kilometer, it leads to an open field where a dilapidated factory sits.

Jude chitters rapidly before flying high up into the air. The rest of us wait for him to do an aerial search. He returns shortly, lands, and shifts into human form.

"I don't see anything."

"Let me hop over and check the windows," Arthur suggests.

He changes into his horny toad and bounds off. Soon, the Scot shifts back and waves us over.

"She's down there!" he hisses in a whisper. "Chained up!"

My eyes narrow at his words.

I might just be an ass, but I'm about to go kick some—nobody hurts Belle.

Chapter 34

Belle

"**G**et ready for me, Breeder," the tiger shifter all but purrs as he saunters up between my spread legs —my skirt is tossed up, but my panties are long gone.

I sputter out a cough.

"Is that it?" I demand.

He rears back, offering me some personal space. A frown mars his face.

"Is what it?" he repeats in confusion.

"That line—is *that* line all I get for foreplay?"

The tiger shifter looks over his shoulder hesitantly at the dean and Dr. Going To Get Stabbed By Me. Dean Hardwick is wearing a smug grin. The scientist looks baffled.

"She's in the throes of heat," the doc insists. "Take her now."

I look at the imbecile askance—this guy's insane.

"I am not in the "throes of heat"—*obviously*," I spit.

The scientist scowls furiously at me for contradicting him.

"I have tested this product time and time again."

"Yeah, well, you tested it wrong," I snap at him.

"Your blood is a perfect match!" he yells in agitation.

I shake my head and let out a pitying sigh before addressing Dean Hardwick.

"Maybe you need to get another scientist?" I suggest to the only one who seems to have any brains in the room— aside from myself.

Dr. Failure gasps in insult before puffing up in importance.

"I am the top of my field; I'll have you know!" he crows..

"Whoa. I thought Dr. Fauci was the top of the field," I cut the mad scientist off—Doc Fauci is the only one I remember seeing on TV.

The shifter scientist looks at me with disgust.

"Those are *human* scientists."

"Well, I bet they could do this shit better than *you're* doing."

The dude lets out an inhuman squawk and lunges at me, but Dean Hardwick holds him back. He's assessing me calculatingly like he did before when we first met.

It's not a good feeling.

The scientist looks like he wants to stab me—well, it's not *my fault* that his stuff doesn't work.

Doc begins pacing in agitation and muttering to himself, "Should work. Blood is a perfect match. All the levels, blah, blah, blah. Scientist talk."

He doesn't actually say that last bit—it's just what I heard.

I snicker. What this idiot man doesn't realize is that I spend every day practically "in heat". His little concoction of whatever isn't going to change anything.

It's like that episode of *Family Guy* where Quagmire gets

choked to death by his sister's boyfriend but he ends up living—*because he chokes himself every night.*

"Go over the numbers again," the dean smoothly commands the scientist.

Dr. Reject clearly doesn't like being told to fix his shit but, considering how I'm not writhing on the floor in absolute wetness, he clearly needs to go reassess things. He stomps out of the room, pouting worse than a toddler who didn't get his way.

Of course, I'm still left tied up, legs spread wide like a whorish sacrifice to the shifter gods.

The tiger is still looking at me lustfully—as are his other two companions.

I just glare back at them.

"Do you want some pointers?" I ask the tiger when he refuses to look away.

"Some pointers for what?" he smirks.

"Foreplay—*making the effort.*"

He raises an eyebrow, "I don't need any of that. I have a giant cock."

Whelp, he's got me there.

Suddenly, the doctor comes rushing back and races over to Dean Hardwick, whispering something frantically in his ear.

Dr. Dipshit looks concerned—*and that's concerning.*

The dean's eyes widen fractionally and lock with mine. I don't like what I see there. It's a mixture of 'oops, we effed up' and 'I can't wait to see what comes of it'. He claps the scientist on the back.

"Well, at least we now know why she's not in heat," Dean Stiffdick says with a smarmy grin in my direction.

I raise a finger in question because I can't raise a hand.

"Ah, I would like to know what's going on, please."

The scientist seems calmer since the dean doesn't appear overly upset over his fuck-up. Doc walks over to me.

"Turns out, I gave you the wrong shot," he explains.

"Excuse me!" I splutter. "What kind of scientist are you?!"

His frown is back in place.

"It was a mistake."

"Yeah—a *rookie* mistake! What the hell did you shoot me up with then?"

Dr. Pilkins tugs at his collar.

"It's an experimental drug."

Great.

Just whatever a woman who's tied up wants to hear.

"And what does this "experimental drug" do?" I prod.

"Changes people into a certain type of shifter."

"Yes," Dean Hardwick adds, stepping forward next to the scientist, and a gleam of fanaticism glows in his eyes. "With this, we can create the ultimate shifter—a one-of-a-kind shifter!"

My eyes widen in awe.

"You're turning me into a unicorn?!"

"Unicorns aren't real," Dr. That I Want To Choke sneers.

"You just told me that you're turning me into something *one-of-a-kind*—that's a unicorn in my language."

"Well, your language is dumb," the doctor retorts.

"Almost as dumb as someone who mixed up the shots?" I parry dryly.

"Children, children!" Dean Boner chuckles, raising both his hands in our direction. "There's no need to quibble. We're going to get along great. Our little Breeder here is going to become something more—and then she can breed us one-of-a-kind shifters!"

I feel my stomach drop even more.

Fuck me.

I just became their unicorn bitch.

Chapter 35

Belle

"Wait!" I call, and everyone freezes at the urgency in my voice. "I need to pee! I mean, I think I might even have the shits, and it'll be like a fountain if we do anal—you know what I mean? Well, I guess we wouldn't be doing anal if you're trying to impregnate me, but it still could come out. . . nobody wants that, right?"

All the men take a hasty step away from me.

At least I have their attention now.

In my nervousness, I babbled a bit—but, in my defense, I think anyone would get the mouth runs in my situation. Not only has the good ol' doc confessed to fucking up but, underneath the surface of my skin, *something is changing.*

I can feel movement, and it makes me want to puke.

"Changed my mind," I say with a gag. "I don't have the squirts, I'm going to vom instead."

I turn my head and, like a class act, puke out the side of my mouth. It dribbles down into my hair, my arm, and onto the floor.

Ew, toad in a hole tastes terrible coming back up—it smells even worse.

It's chunkier than Campbell's soup, and it's slipping down the inside of my arm. It's enough to make me gag and retch some more. I start choking, and doc quickly steps forward.

Big mistake—I wasn't done barfing yet.

I spew chunks in his face. It coats his glasses, and some might have gone into his mouth. He screams—which is stupid—since what was on his lip now falls into his mouth.

He stumbles back into one of the other shifters—who knocks into another shifter. Instantly, a brawl breaks out. Dean Stiffdick just stands there with an exasperated look on his face.

"Enough!" he snaps. "Dr. Pilkins, go clean yourself up. You three, go get something to clean her up. I have to make a phone call."

He pinches the bridge of his nose like everything is just too much for him.

Fucker has no one to blame but himself.

He shoos everyone from the room. The sound of the door thudding and locking securely behind them echoes around the room. I sit there, coated in my own vomit, wondering how I came to be here.

Then again, as a sex addict, I probably shouldn't be surprised I'm strapped to a table with my legs spread and no underwear on.

I try to concentrate on something other than the feel of my puke sliding down my arm—it's itchy, cold, and gross.

Well, it's *cooling.*

I wiggle to escape it and try to rub it off, but find that it's acting as the nastiest lubricant known to man. It Criscos my hand until I can shimmy it painfully from the rope.

Yes!

Freed by my own puke!

Take that, bad guys!

I bring my hand up to my nose and inhale with a big whiff. It's like all my senses are heightened, and I can smell things a thousand percent more than I could before. My barf wafts up into my nostrils, and I instantly keel over and retch all over my left wrist.

Bull's eye!

Direct shot!

Puke spews through my mouth and in between the rope and my skin. Quickly, I wiggle my left arm free.

Now, just to get my feet.

Holding my nose, because I really don't want to smell it anymore and keep puking, I sling the vomit down at my ankles. My feet are harder to get through the tough knots—even lubed up—and I end up scraping myself severely.

But, finally, I get free.

I look around the room frantically looking for an escape route when my gaze snags on a dirty window. Through the grime, I see a familiar face peering through the window.

It's Arthur—my horny toad knight in shining armor.

Chapter 36

Theo

THE SLIPPERY DICK

"What the fuck have they done to her?" Jack wonders as we stare down at Belle through a small dusty window.

She appears to be the only one in the room, and her arms are coated in a sickly-looking orange substance.

"I don't know, but we need to get her out of here, though," Jude says, looking around vigilantly.

"I'll stay behind," Jack offers. "You know I can't enter."

We all nod. His ass is too big to fit through the window, but a cockchafer, a slippery Dick, and a horny toad can easily fit. I nudge the window open, and Jude quickly shifts and flies in. Arthur shifts and follows suit.

I'm the last to go.

It's tricky being a water animal and *not* shifting into water. I can easily die if I don't shift back into my human form in time. Being soft bodied and free falling through a window into a building, I can easily land on something and pierce myself—but Jude knows the drill and will catch me.

Hopefully.

Taking a deep breath, I quickly shift into my fish and drop through the window. Not shifting in water is like having an out of body experience—and it's not a very pleasant one. As soon as Jude catches me, I instantly morph back into my human form, greedily sucking down air.

We're all naked—except for Belle, who I can now smell is covered in vomit. Her ankles are bleeding, and I can faintly scent the metallic tang of blood, a more subtle odor underneath the stench of vomit.

"Poor lass, what happened to you?" Arthur croons, walking right up to her, not bothered by the smell or appearance of vomit.

Belle's shaking violently and doesn't answer him.

"We need to get out of here now—before the Tershes return," I prod.

Belle nods, on board with Plan Get the Hell Out of Dodge—the only problem is she's too big to fit through the escape route.

"What are we going to do?" I ask Jude, who I know is already thinking the same thing.

"She's going to have to go through the only exit available for her," Jude responds. "You and Arthur need to go back through the window, though."

I stare at him.

It's almost impossible to do unless he tosses me back up and out it. From the look on his face—that's Jude's plan.

"No," I disagree firmly. "We're in this together. I know I'm just a fish, but I can help!"

Jude's face softens.

"I didn't mean it like that—"

"I know you didn't," I cut him off, "but I'm not going anywhere."

"And neither am I," says Arthur. "As Theo said—we're in this together. Jack will cover our asses once we get out there. Sian and Elise are waiting at the cousin's flat and will meet us somewhere on campus. Once we return, we're going to get the hell out of here."

"Will I have time to shower?" Belle wonders absently.

I try not to chuckle.

"Let's just concentrate on getting out of here; ok, love?"

Suddenly, Jude stiffens.

"Quick—shift!" he commands. "Someone's coming!"

I change instantly, without question, because I trust Jude implicitly. He and Arthur also shift. On a stroke of genius, Belle rushes over and slops some puke on each of us.

The clever woman not only has masked our scent, but she's helped hydrate me—even if it is minging[1].

Not a moment too soon, Jude buzzes off, and Arthur hops into hiding. Belle steps in front of me. Hopefully, whoever it is leaves soon because I need air.

Stat.

The door opens and two Tertiaries stroll into the room.

Instantly, Belle straightens up.

"Dean Hardwick let me up. He demands that I refresh myself—he wants a filthy whore only metaphorically."

The Tershes don't even question her lie.

"Here, we brought you some towels. Clean yourself up," the one shifter snaps at Belle, tossing her some cloths.

"Ewwww, gross! I'm not just wiping this off of me—I want a shower!" she snaps right back.

"We don't have time for this," the other shifter decrees. "Dean Hardwick—"

"I don't give *a fuck* about Dean Hardwick!" Belle interrupts. "I might be some American whore to you, but I have principles—and one of them is that I don't screw *covered in puke.* So, either you arrange a shower for me with the shampoo that I need for my hair to make sure that the color doesn't fade, or else I'm not spreading these legs willingly."

"Who says it has to be willingly?" the first shifter asks.

I see red at this transparent threat to rape Belle.

My intense rage makes me lose focus, and I accidentally shift back into a human. Instantly, the two men change into their animal forms—a black mamba and Komodo dragon.

I panic and shift back into a fish—which is probably the dumbest thing I could ever have done because now I'm just a sitting duck, er, flopping fish, waiting to die.

The black mamba races forward, stretches out, and strikes with its fangs protruding. I lurch into the air helplessly, and Belle screams. With a preternatural speed, she grabs a nearby folding chair, darts forward, and bashes the snake out of the way with it.

"Nobody eats my slippery dick!" she screams.

Over and over, Belle smacks the snake with her weapon of choice.

The other shifter seems stunned at what's going on. He advances upon her cautiously—but doesn't attack—and I realize that she must be an asset Dean Hardwick is not willing to lose.

When the black mamba stops moving, Belle rounds on the Komodo dragon. He gives her a feral snarl, but doesn't do much more.

Belle, on the other hand, does.

She chases after the giant lizard all around the room. I quickly shift back into my human form and glance around the room. It's lined with counters, littered with scrap yard[2]. I quickly grab a bag, throw it around the snake, and tie it as tightly as I can.

There's a good chance if the Tersh shifts back into a human, he'll break the bag. The black mamba writhes inside angrily as I stuff the bag into an open trash can and drop the lid back on—that should hold him a little better.

Jude and Arthur have since shifted back into their human forms, but the tertiary pays none of us any attention as he's too busy dealing with Belle.

The Komodo dragon darts toward the door and transforms halfway into a human to open it, but Belle advances upon him with an animalistic ferocity. She screams something about being with WWE and smacks him over the head soundly.

A sickening crunch echoes around the room and the Tersh drops to the ground. Unconscious, his body fully takes on his human form. Satisfied with herself, Belle tosses the folding chair down and fluffs her hair.

"Let's get the fuck out of here," she spits.

I look over at Jude and Arthur, who are wearing the same stunned looks—*but we don't need to be told twice.*

We race down a darkened corridor, hoping that we don't meet with anyone else. By some miracle of God, we make it outside. Jack is already there waiting, changed into his ass.

"Get on Jack's back!" Jude yells at Belle as he shifts back into his cockchafer.

Arthur transforms into his animal, and I jump on Jack's back behind Belle.

"Go!" I yell.

Like the noblest of steeds, Jack takes off. We hear the savage roar of a Tertiary and know that we don't have long to get back to our vehicle.

Jude buzzes out of sight, the wind carrying him at a faster speed to our car. From my periphery, I see Arthur running alongside Jack. He's easily keeping pace with the donkey—who's legging it[3] down the lane.

Another vicious howl rends the air, and I feel Belle tense under my arms wrapped tightly around her.

"It's ok—don't look back," I command—more to myself than to her.

"Ahhhhhhhhh!" Belle shrieks so high I think she might pierce my ear drums. "I looked back! Fucking Shere Khan is chasing us!"

Thank Heavens Rudyard Kipling was a Brit. For once, I know what Belle is talking about—but I wish that I didn't because a tiger can easily outpace an ass.

Especially one carrying two humans—even if they're bred to be pack animals, they weren't bred to hunt down their prey.

But tigers are.

And this bastard is almost on our arses.

Jack starts swerving and braying in fear, his animal side taking over. He zigzags to the left abruptly, and the motion dumps Belle and me off. Together, we tumble to the ground in a heap.

I grab her head swiftly and flatten us, nose into the dirt. Jack is kicking uncontrollably in his mulish angst. Finally gathering enough courage, I look up to see the tiger leisurely strolling toward us.

It's keeping a wary eye on Jack's ass but, otherwise, doesn't seem concerned.

I try to shove Belle behind me, but she keeps smacking my hands away and rolls on top of me. I realize that the daft woman is shielding me from the advancing Tersh.

"Belle, get off—"

My shaky order is silenced by the loud bellow of Jude—

once again human—as he jumps over Belle's and my prone forms. In his hand is a giant dead tree branch that he's lit on fire.

The bloody genius.

I could kiss him.

Jude lands nimbly in front of us and brandishes the homemade torch at the huge cat. I can see the twin flames reflected in the feline's large eyes—which have grown bigger with fear at the sight.

"Arthur! Bring round the saloon!" Jude directs the toad.

He never stops looking at the tiger, though. Methodically, he inches forward, shaking the fiery stick at the Tertiary. In return, the cat slowly slinks back.

It doesn't take long for Arthur to drive up. He hops out and rushes over to Jack, who is still kicking in abject fear. Thankfully, Arthur manages to calm down the ass and coax Jack to shift. I rush Belle over to the car, and she surprises me by taking the wheel.

"Get in," she grinds out.

I quickly scoot over so that Arthur and Jack can pile in.

"Er, Belle, are you sure this is the time—" Arthur starts, but Belle just revs the engine in answer.

Jude looks back. Jack has the passenger door still open, and he's waving frantically for him to get in. Lunging once more at the tiger, Jude throws the flaming branch at the cat and flees into the safety of the vehicle.

Belle whips it into drive and guns the gas. Instantly, we shoot forward. The crazy woman plows over the burning hunk of wood and barrels right into the tiger. The Tersh screams and attempts to scamper out of the way, but can't.

He's scooped up onto the bonnet until Belle flips a u-ey. Then, the cat goes flying and knocks hard into a nearby tree trunk. She rights the tiny vehicle once more and races away down the road.

I glance back once in the side mirror.

The Tersh is still immobile—but the tiger's flashing eyes promise revenge.

Chapter 37
Belle

"Get out of the way, you bloody wankin' sods!" Jack screams at the car meandering slowly in front of us.

He lays on the horn, but the car just goes slower.

Jack zips past him, beyond pissed—maybe I shouldn't have switched places will him, but he knows these roads better than me.

Also, I kept diving on the wrong side of the road.

I'm upset—cut me some slack.

"Do you want me to flip him off?" I offer, keen on doing something.

Arthur just shakes his head.

"No, we need to focus. I've texted the girls to meet us on campus. We need to get your passport and get you to the airport."

"What about my stuff?"

I really don't want anyone seeing—or handling—all my, er, toys.

"I'm sorry, but you need to get out of here *now*."

I look down at my hands—every single nail is chipped.

Those bastards ruined my nail job.

"Where's your passport at?" Arthur continues.

"I don't know. Let me think."

"Think quickly, love," Jude urges. "We have very little time to pick up the girls and get off campus. We can text Elise and Sian where your passport is. They can get it and we can leave sooner."

"Ummmm. . . " I trial off, my brain shutting down because I need it to do actual work. "I'm sorry! I can't remember!"

"It's ok," Theo soothes. "You've been through a traumatic experience. It's just that we're in a car, but everyone else is running."

"What's that mean?" I wonder.

"It means," Jack elucidates, passing another car, "that we have to follow where the road goes—but animals can go as the crow flies."

"Wait—all you guys are crows?" I blurt out in even more confusion.

Jude lets out a strained chuckled.

"No, it means that the Tershes chasing us don't have to follow the traffic signs, speed zones, the physical path of the road. They can run through the woods and make short cuts—"

"It means that they can get to Oxford faster," Jack interrupts for clarification.

"Oh. . . oh!" I exclaim when I finally get what they're stepping in—and it's a shit sandwich.

Think, brain, think—where's my passport?

"I remember!" I yell triumphantly. "It's inside my box of butt plugs, under the user manual!"

Jude coughs.

"Butt plugs come with a user's manual?" he queries.

"Of course! You shove that sucker in wrong, and you could be walking sideways for a week—not to mention if you shove it up too far into the rectal abyss. I've heard true horror stories of people needing to surgically remove things that got stuck up there."

"Right," Jude says solemnly. "And this butt plug box is where?"

"In the hall closet underneath my container of flavored lubes. Oh, tell Sian and Elise to grab the small white bottle. It's piña colada flavored. I need a drink after the shit I've seen."

"Is it. . . alcoholic?" Arthur asks, scratching his dark red beard.

"Not sure—there might be booze in it."

"And you're just going to *drink it*?" Jude prompts.

"Well, I would prefer to slurp it off of someone's cock, but no one offered."

The four men—including Jack—turn to stare at me.

"Just have them pick it up," I sigh.

Airports allow me two ounces or less of carry-on liquid, and I'm going to capitalize on this golden opportunity.

Arthur texts the girls and waits until his phone dings with a response.

"Fuck," he curses.

I startle—I've never heard Arthur use that word before.

It's super hot with his Scottish accent.

"What's wrong now," I sigh.

"Elise says that your entire flat is taped off and there are bizzies everywhere," Arthur announces.

"Fuck is right," Jack agrees, running a hand through his grayish brown hair.

"Dean Hardwick must have sent somebody—that man

really has it out for me, and all because I *wouldn't* sleep with his men!"

The *fucking* irony, right?

"Can't Sian or Elise fly in?" I suggest.

"Sian's titmouse is smaller and flies better—maybe she could get the passport, but it would be difficult for her to get in and out," Arthur mumbles. "Jude would be better suited since he's the smallest and can crawl through cracks and holes."

"Then, we'll send Jude in once we get to campus," I decree.

"That still isn't the solution. Even if Jude enters your flat because he's an inconspicuous insect, he would still have to shift back into a human to take your passport—*a naked human*. Don't you think that would set off some proverbial alarms?" Arthur jokes.

"Honestly, any other day, I really don't think anyone would blink," I laugh.

The four men exchange a look.

"I kind of forgot that that was normal for you," Jack jokes. "*Not* that I'm judging!" he quickly adds.

"I think Jude is our best option," I insist. "We just need to create a diversion around my apartment building so he can get up there—*and out with my passport*. As long as there's plenty of people around, I would think that we will be safe. . . I mean, it would be pretty strange if a tiger attacked us midday at Oxford University, right?"

"That's what we thought before you got nabbed," Theo counters.

"Yeah, but I was an idiot and walked away—out of sight —from people," I argue.

"She's right," Arthur concurs.

"Hey—did you just call me an idiot?!" I ask in affront.

Arthur smirks.

"Nay, lass—*you did*. I was just agreeing, and not even with that bit. As long as we have people around with all their phones, we should be ok. People record everything nowadays—Tershes won't want to expose themselves. What kind of diversion were you thinking?"

"Something obnoxious—like me streaking," I suggest.

"Streaking?" Jude repeats.

"Yeah, ya know, running around naked in public."

"You want to jot around campus *starkers*?!" he exclaims.

"You've never done that before?" Jack asks in surprise.

I glare at him.

"No! Just because I have whorish tendencies doesn't mean. . .ok, I don't know where I was going with that argument. It sounded better in my head. Anywho, I think me flashing all of Oxford my lady bits will be sufficiently distracting. But what's the point? Dean Hardwick has to have my file—he knows that I'm American. He knows where I live. Where will we hide? I can't go back home. And what if Dean Stiffdick uses my family against me?! I guess the question is. . .what's it matter if I'm dead or alive?"

"Don't say that!" Arthur snaps harshly. "Never say that you being alive doesn't matter! You living is. . .it's *everything*."

I blink, startled by the depth of his words.

"But a life in hiding is not a life," I argue. "I understand that my survival is important to you—but I don't want to survive to just be on the run the rest of my life. And, now, you're caught up in this mess, forever on the run with me. I've *ruined* your lives!"

Jack rolls his eyes.

"Such melodrama! Are you saying that you'd rather be dead? And you haven't "ruined" our lives—" Jack starts.

"You've enriched them," Theo concludes.

I smile softly at his touching words.

"Listen, we're in this together," Jude reassures me. "We're a team, and we'll figure it out as one."

"A team?" I test.

"A team," Arthur reiterates.

I snort, even though my heart clenches—what a team we make.

Quite the motley crew, but I wouldn't have it any other way.

Chapter 38

Belle

"*B*izzies *are* everywhere!" Arthur breathes when we finally pull on to campus.

Frankly, I don't even care—I'm just relieved that we even made it there without getting stopped by a tiger and slashed to death.

I don't say this out loud because tensions are already pretty high in the car.

After our heartfelt moment, things went back to the way they were—rife with anxiety.

Jack pulls into student parking just as Elise and Sian text that they've arrived.

"I told them to meet us here," Arthur mumbles. "If they can even find us in the melee."

"Well, we don't have time to waste. We need to get our diversion on and get my passport—wait, what about you guys? Do you have your passports?!"

"We'll sneak onto the plane as our animals; don't worry about us," Theo soothes.

How the fuck is a fish going to sneak onto a plane?!

189

"I feel like there's a fatal flaw in your plan, but baby steps. One thing at a time. Time for Operation Campus Streaking."

"I'm not completely on board with this plan," Jude says unenthusiastically. "How about I quickly go scope things out as a cockchafer?"

"What if the bad guys are waiting at my apartment, though?"

"I will smell—fuck, no I won't. I forgot that for some reason we can't smell those bastards anymore."

A lightbulb goes off in my head.

"Dr. Fuckface—the scientist who used an experimental drug on me—said he found a way to mask shifters' scents!"

All the guys start talking at one.

"Dr. Fuckface?"

"An experimental drug?!"

"They can mask our scents?!"

"Motherfucker!"

I laugh. Of course, Theo is confused by my name for the evil scientist. Jude and Arthur ask the important questions, and Jack—he gets it all and just sums it up in that one perfect word.

"And—Dean Hardwick *knows* about you guys."

"How so?" Jude prompts.

"He knows that you're Primaries."

"Interesting," Arthur hums.

God, he's weird.

"Ok, being here is not safe—who knows where the dean or that boffin[1] are. I'm going to get your passport and we're going to get out of here as fast as we can—but I don't want you running around starkers. We need a different diversion."

"Don't worry, mate—I've got your back," Jack grins. "I have the perfect diversion."

Why do I feel like me streaking is the saner—and safer —option?

"Theo and Arthur—stay with Belle. Elise and Sian will be here soon. Hopefully, Sian's cousin's vehicle can fit us better than this dinky thing. I'll return shortly. Jack—work your magic."

With that, Jude strips and shifts.

I swear to God I'll never get used to this man taking off his clothes—and turning into a freaking bug.

Jack follows suit. It's amazing how quickly he transforms —in the blink of an eye. I kind of want to film him and watch it happen in slow motion. The donkey brays at me, and I smack his ass while laughing at the irony.

"Get going, diversion," I joke. "Operation Asstastic is now in motion!"

Jack quirks an ear and blows a raspberry at me before trotting off. Moments later, Sian and Elise show up. I hug them tightly, so thankful to see them again.

"Are you all right?" Sian asks with concern.

"What happened?!" Elise cries. "You smell terrible."

"Sorry, that's my puke. It's a long story—a really long story. I haven't even told the guys yet. Let's get out of here, and I'll tell you what happened."

"What are we going to do in the meantime?" Sian wonders.

"We should get around a crowd—there's safety in numbers," Arthur directs.

"Um, ok, then we should go to the center quad—there's always people there... unless the cops are looking for *me*."

"If they're working for the dean, they might be," Theo worries.

He ducks into the car and comes back out with a hat.

"Put this cap on—it should cover your hair and help to disguise you better."

Dammit—I forgot about my unicorn hair, but I'd rather shave it off than get caught and become someone's unicorn bitch.

We make our way to the main area of campus where people study, eat, and relax. It's bustling with students, but I still feel on edge. Suddenly, there's loud shouting across the way. The crowd breaks and campus security comes running into view.

It looks like they're chasing someone. . .

I squint.

Or something—*namely, a donkey.*

"Looks like Operation Asstsatic is going well," I joke.

Arthur narrows his eyes.

"Shite—Jack's got the passport. I can see it in his mouth. Come on, Theo! Girls, stay here!"

"Wait—" I call, but the two men are already off.

"I don't like this," Elise mumbles.

"Me, neither. The more we get separated, the worse," I concur.

The three of us keep an attentive eye on our surroundings as the seconds tick by—which, soon, turn into minutes.

"Do you see anything?" Sian whines in frustration.

She's quite a bit shorter than Elise and me.

"Not yet," Elise answers. "Hold on—there's Jack again! But where are Theo and Arthur?!"

I look to where she's pointing.

Sure enough, I see the familiar shaggy beast that's Jack's ass running back into the quad. The same two campus guards are chasing him, but my favorite fish and toad are nowhere in sight.

Suddenly, Elise lets out a horrified shriek.

"They have tranquilizing guns!" she cries.

"What?" I cry, more in confusion than fear.

"They're used to put animals under!" Sian says fearfully. "We have to help Jack!"

The three of us lock eyes and nod—*looks like the 'little women' are going to save the men.*

As a unit, we race forward, leaping over students and even shoving them out of our way. When we catch up to Jack and the guards, we're a ways from the quad and the crowds. The two men have Jack cornered and are holding *a taser.*

Without thinking, I leap between them and the donkey.

"Hey!" I scream, holding out both my hands in front of me at campus security.

They both freeze, unsure as to what I'm yelling about— hell, I don't even know. It's not like I have a plan. Dammit! I knew we should have done Operation Bare Ass *my* way, not Jack's.

Buuuuuuuut. . .

I might still have the perfect diversion tactic up my wizard's sleeve.

And F.Y.I.—I totally meant that to be dirty, not mystical.

"Miss, please watch out!" The stern guard berates. "That's a wild animal behind you."

"It's an ass," I point out dryly.

"Their kicks can be fatal," he counters with a frown.

Jesus, this dude is a real stick in the mud.

"If you're worried about "wild" asses. . . then, watch this!"

Making sure campus security is still focused on me, I whip off my tank top. Honestly, it's a relief since the damned thing stunk so much. I caress my boobs provocatively over the black lace of my bra.

The two guards' eyes bulge—I *definitely* have their attention.

I continue to touch myself before I saunter over to Elise and Sian—who are staring at me like I've gone insane.

"Play along," I whisper when I stroll up Sian.

"Wha—"

"Operation Wild Ass Diversion is about to start—sorry about how bad I smell," I apologize in advance.

With that, I pull the shorter woman into my arms and kiss her deeply.

Chapter 39

Sian
THE TITMOUSE

*B*elle's soft tongue sneaks out between her lips to tangle with mine, and I gasp in surprise—well, *more* surprise. But, as far as diversion tactics go, this one is brilliant. I can feel the heavy stares of campus security boring into the two of us.

The bold Yank tugs me even closer, her hands sweeping down the sides of my tits and ribcage. Her mouth masterfully snogs mine, and I'm swept up in a rush of arousal knowing that Elise is watching.

I lean in and nip the bottom of Belle's lip to let her know that I'm keen for more. The brilliant woman immediately responds by gripping my hips and rubbing her tits against mine in sure, thorough side strokes. The methodical movement tantalizes me, and my nipples stiffen under my bra.

Belle lets out a breathy moan, as does Elise, and I smile against the Yank's mouth—I love that we're making my girlfriend burn. I inch my fingers down Belle's stomach to the waistband of her skirt.

"Do it," Belle whispers.

I pull back to look into her bright blue eyes, so different from my brown ones. Over her shoulder, the guards watch us in utter fascination. I'm too turned on to worry about Jack any longer—hopefully, he's taken his cue and escaped.

To my right, I can see Elise grinning.

I dip my fingers into Belle's elastic and rest them there while raising a questioning brow at my girlfriend. She tosses me a wink of encouragement—before stepping up and joining.

Together, we slip a hand inside Belle's skirt.

ELISE the BOOBY

I stare down into my girlfriend's warm brown eyes. Her face is flushed with arousal, and I can imagine how the color matches her muff.

When I turn to Belle, I forget for a moment that she's taller than Sian. Her eyes are nearly level with mine. Her brightly colored hair fans around her shoulders, creating a rainbow halo around her fair face.

Her blue eyes are wide with excitement—Belle is definitely into exhibitionism.

As are Sian and me.

I link a pinky with Sian as we dive inside Belle's skirt. She's not wearing any knickers, and I love the feel of her smooth shaved skin. Together, Sian and I teasingly dance around her pussy.

Belle pulls me in for a kiss. The taste of her chapstick is sweet against my tongue. Sian stares up at us, nearly panting—the guards make a similar sound.

"Let's make her fanny flutter," I smirk at Sian, who nods in agreement.

We dip a finger dip into Belle's pussy, and she gasps loudly. Anyone with eyes can clearly see that we're poking her in broad daylight. Belle is deliciously wet and ready.

I'm gutted that this is just a diversion—*for now*.

Now that I know the Yank and my girlfriend are game, we will be finishing this at a later time. Unfortunately, our little diversion is almost up.

Jack is long gone, and time is precious.

Reluctantly, I pull my hand back, as does Sian. Belle scowls and rocks her hips forward, but I nip her lip in warning.

"Another time," I promise.

Together, we turn to the guards.

I almost burst into laughter. Both men are sporting giant stonkers[1].

Mission accomplished.

Chapter 40

Belle

"Sorry 'bout your boners!" I giggle as the girls and I run from campus security.

It's not cool to give someone blue balls—but desperate times call for no orgasms.

Elise, Sian, and I only make it about twenty yards before the guards shake out of their trance and start to chase us.

"Hey, wait! You can't do that in public!" the stern guy shouts at us.

"Where did that donkey go?" the other one pants.

We race back to the student parking lot to find Jude, Jack, Arthur, and Theo waiting for us next to the car we escaped in. Both Jude and Jack are in human form, once more, and clothed—which is a total let down.

"Did you see that ass that ran by?" Jack tosses out nonchalantly to no one in particular. "Rather odd to see a wild animal like that on campus."

Campus security comes to a screeching halt at these words, seemingly forgetting about us ladies.

"Which way did it go?" Boss Guard demands.

Jack points randomly behind him.

"Took off in that direction—toward the cafeteria."

Boss Guard cusses loudly.

"Come on, Wes, we better get over there before that bloody thing tears the kitchens apart and the university makes us redundant[1]?!"

Together, the two of them dash off.

Honestly, I'm a bit miffed that the girls' and my performance didn't get a little more attention.

I lock eyes with Jack, and his gaze *burns* into mine.

"That was some diversion," he growls.

I blow him a kiss—*his pants can't hide the real estate that he's pack in there from our 'show'.*

"Best diversion yet!" I crow.

"And I've got the best solution!" Sian cries triumphantly, looking at her phone. "Quick—everyone into the saloon!"

"What saloon?"

"The car!" she clarifies as the others all scramble in.

I wait to squeeze in after the girls when a sound catches my attention. Staring into the darkness underneath a nearby car, I swear eyes stare back at me.

Elise pulls my hand to get in. I look at her and back again—but the sun dances behind a cloud, and I realize it was just a shadow. Moving quickly, I hop into the cramped vehicle.

"Ugh, this thing *has* turned into a freaking clown car again."

"Clown car?" Theo wonders.

"Yeah—ya know, those small-ass cars in the circus that they cram full of seventy clowns—that's what this is like."

Jude sits behind the wheel, ready to go.

"If it gets us out of here, who cares if we're squished?" he shrugs. "Sian—what's this ace solution?"

"My cousin texted me—"

"The shady one?" Jack asks.

"Yep—the very one—he can sneak us onto a ship going south."

"So, we didn't need my passport after all?" I whine.

"It doesn't hurt to have it, love" Arthur argues.

"Plus, we got off together," Elise adds.

"Hold the phone—who got off?!" I shout.

"Um, the three of us," Sian says, pointing at herself, Elise, and me.

I pout.

Making out with them was magical as fuck, but I sure as shit didn't 'gasm!

"What's wrong?" Theo murmurs, sensing my inner angst.

"Nothing," I mumble.

"Liar," Jack prods, and I stick my tongue out at him.

"I think we have more important things to focus on, but if you must know. . . I'm sulking because Elise and Sian got off, and I didn't," I admit.

"What are you talking about?" Sian frowns. "We all got off."

"I can promise you that I didn't!"

"Hun, how can you say that?" Elise chimes in.

Jude holds up a hand.

"Belle—to get off means to snog and fondle someone."

"And snogging is kissing," Arthur further elucidates.

I let their words sink in and just tip my head back and laugh.

"Well, don't go to America and tell people how you 'got off'—that means 'you came' over there."

The tiny car packed with bodies falls silent before we all erupt into peals of laughter.

"Another time, we'll 'get off' your way," Sian promises, and I shudder.

I look forward to that day.

"So, where south is this ship going?" I toss out, bringing us back on topic.

"Dunno," Sian shrugs.

"It doesn't matter because we're going to jump ship, anyway," Jude announces.

I almost swallow my tongue.

"I hope that's another idiom I don't understand," I grimace.

"Not at all," Jude denies. "Sian's cousin can get us on the ship, but the Tershes will still be able to track us to the docks and look up what ship left port. But, if we jump ship —and either swim or get on another—we can buy ourselves some more time. It will be harder for the Tertiaries to find water shifters to help them track us."

"Harder, but not impossible," Arthur counters.

"I know, but it will help us buy some time until we can disappear completely," Jude responds.

"And how are we going to ever 'completely disappear'?" I ask.

No one answers me.

We fall into a tense silence.

The drive to the docks takes about an hour—Jack drives like a madman, but he gets us there in one piece.

"There!" Sian cries. "There's our ship! Harri said to mention his name when we board is all."

"Sounds too easy," I whisper.

This is the part in the story where the bad guys always catch the good guys and slit their throats.

A hand flies to my neck at the thought—I have no desire to become Nearly Headless Nick.

And what if the tiger misses my throat and gets my tits instead?!

I'll be Boobless Belle—forever forced to wear baggy shirts with a neckline up to my ears.

I blurt out this new, albeit deep-seated, fear, but they just chuckle.

"I won't deny we're in serious peril, but unless they've hacked Sian's phone..." Jude trails off.

"They've made a drug that can change people into shifters—I doubt hacking phones is a problem for them!"

Jack nearly swerves into another car.

"You never told us that part!" he yells.

"I haven't told you the half of it!" I screech right back.

"Park here," Jude commands. "Everyone out—I need to shift and check out the ship."

"What if they're there, and you can't smell them?" I remind.

"I should be able to tell who they are from before," he theorizes.

I don't point out a new shifter could be aboard.

We're running out of options.

Jude steps out of the car and to the side, out of view from the bustling port. He shifts and zips off. The rest of us all huddle together, our backs pressed together tightly.

Suddenly, I feel like I'm being watched.

I narrow my eyes and squint against the bright light of the sun. Spinning around, I search in a circle, but don't see anything amiss.

"Get back in formation," Arthur barks like a military leader.

"Yes, sir," I joke, saluting him before protecting my back again.

It's then that I see it—a pair of familiar eyes staring.

The same eyes I thought I saw before under the car.

They blink and lurch forward as the creature saunters out of the darkened corner of a warehouse building.

"Guys—wh-wh-what's that?" I ask, pointing a shaky finger at a semi-familiar looking animal.

"Fuck," Jack curses. "It's the Secondary that saw Jude."

Oh.

So this is what a jackal looks like—I remember now, just like I remember the thing *winking* at me.

dramatic sigh

I knew this was too easy.

Chapter 41

Belle

"What's that red stuff all over its muzzle?" I talk out loud.

"Blood," Theo supplies.

"You don't know that—maybe it's ketchup!" I counter in denial.

"It's not," Arthur bursts my bubble.

"Wait—he's just a Secondary? That's not bad, right?"

"If he's not with a pack, he's not as deadly, but think about dogs—would you want one attacking you?"

"Are we talking a Rottweiler or a Chihuahua? I mean, Chihuahuas can be nasty little shits, but I wouldn't go against a Weiler."

"Well, jackals are bigger than Chihuahuas, but meaner than Rottweilers," Arthur supplies.

I blanch and look hastily around for an escape.

"Too bad we aren't monkeys," I wish.

"You want to throw shit at the jackal?" Jack muses.

I laugh, in spite of myself.

"No! So we could climb up the buildings!"

"That makes more sense," Elise smirks. "But I bet the Secondary would run if we threw excrement at it."

The jackal snarls—apparently, it's close enough to hear us and doesn't like our not-a-real plan.

When the four-legged menace is about twenty feet away, a strange chittering sound fills the air. A small insect starts buzzing around the jackal, who yelps and dashes back into the shadows.

The bug flies over to us and swiftly turns into a naked Jude.

Yum, Nude Jude—sounds like a deliciously naughty British dessert that I want to gobble up.

"Here's your stuff," Jack says, giving Jude his clothes.

He quickly dresses, but the jackal from the shadows doesn't.

From the obscurity, steps a man whose skin matches the darkness. He's gorgeous, hung, and when he smiles—red stains his teeth.

Definitely not ketchup.

"I told you that I was going to squash you, bug," the jackal shifter taunts Jude. "And I'm going to mount your girl."

An irrational flair of jealousy explodes inside of me.

Jude has a girlfriend?

"I promise you I'm nothing more than a *bug*," he spits, "but you'll never lay a finger on Belle!"

"I'm your girlfriend?" I blurt out in wonder.

Sian and Elise laugh, and Jude looks sheepish.

"Er, no, I just know he meant you," he explains.

I smile—it's amazing how I can even feel such joyous emotions when I'm likely to die any second.

"What did you do to him when he was a jackal that made him back up?" I ask Jude.

"I sprayed him—cockchafers have a foul-smelling scent that they use to escape predators."

Too bad this asshole didn't catch me on a Taco Bell day —I could have wiped him out in one fart.

"But it's not enough to deter him forever," Jude continues.

"We just need to get on the ship," Theo urges.

The clamorous sound of a boat horn echoes around us at his words.

"Oh, no—the ship's getting ready to leave!" Sian cries in panic.

"Let's go, bug," the jackal taunts, still a distance from us. "Or do you just give up now? Why don't you just hand over your American tart while you still have all six of your legs?"

Theo's face reddens in anger.

"Don't call Belle that—she's not a tart!"

"Actually, I don't mind—tarts are delicious. My granny used to make them all the time. Cherry's my favorite," I tell him.

"Tart means whore," Elise coughs.

"Oh. . . well, in that case, he's not exactly wrong," I cringe. "But, thank you, you beautiful man. I appreciate you defending my, er, honor."

The jackal doubles over at my words.

"She admits it! I bet her clunge is wider than the Thames!"

At these words, Theo snaps; he rushes the shifter and tackles him to the ground. It's interesting to see since the jackal shifter is large and more muscular—but Theo is faster.

"Girls, get on the ship!" Jude snaps. "I didn't see or sense anyone! It's our only chance—go!"

"No—" I start, but Sian grabs my hand and yanks me away.

Elise follows, and we rush up the plank.

"Harri sent us," Sian pants.

The man checking tickets looks both ways before ushering aboard. Honestly, I doubt Sian even needed to name drop. When three hot women come running up, the club doors usually open wide.

We rush to the rail, but the buildings block our view of the guys.

"We need to hunker down in a room," Elise directs. "Come on."

A young deck hand points to where we can go rest—or hide, in our case. After about thirty minutes, there's a loud commotion above. I want to poke my head out and investigate, but Elise bolts the cabin door shut and props the dresser against.

I don't point out that I doubt this would stop something like a tiger.

The boisterous sounds die down, but my heart continues to beat wildly. It takes everything to not break down, but I don't want to place that burden on the girls—I know they are just as scared.

Suddenly, there's a loud pounding on the door.

"Password!" a familiar voice shouts.

Sian grins.

"Password!" she parrots.

"Satin buttholes!" the voice sings.

Instantly, Elise gets up and shoves the dresser out of the way to open the door. Standing there are Jude, Arthur, and Jack—whose voice I heard. Elise tugs them in and re-slams the door shut before shoving the dresser back in place.

"I've searched this boat top to bottom—I promise we're safe," Jude murmurs to her.

"Um, what's satin buttholes and where's Theo?" I ask.

I'm clinging to Jack and Arthur while trying to figure out how to get Jude closer so I can hold him, too.

"It's the password we devised to ensure it was us," Jack explains.

"It's ridiculous," I giggle-sniffle—that's when you laugh and cry at the same time.

Sometimes, embarrassing snot bubbles pop out of your nose but, luckily, that doesn't happen to me.

Yet.

"And Theo?" I prod.

I feel the guys tense under my touch and the air traps inside my lungs.

"He... didn't make it," Jude confesses.

Both Elise and Sian gasp, but it's nothing compared to the ugly jarring sobs that escape me—I don't even care about the massive snot bubbles forming from my nostrils.

"Theo's gone?" I wail.

There's no consoling me, and no one tries—*we're all trapped in our own ugly worlds of grief and despair.*

I excuse myself to use the bathroom.

No amount of T.P. seems capable of dealing with the mess leaking from my nose. Dammit—where's my purse when I need it most? A couple of tampons would have fixed this problem instantly.

I sit down on the toilet and try to calm myself.

My attempt fails when the water beneath me comes bubbling up and starts splashing onto my ass. I scream and jump off the pot.

Oh, God—it's like those stories you read about on the

internet where snakes come out of the toilets and eat people.

Except these snakes are really humans who want to fuck me for their own nefarious pleasure.

Jude barges into the tiny bathroom labeled W.C.. It can barely fit me, let alone the two of us. My skirt is at my ankles, and I'm sans undies since Dean Raper stole them—I assume.

"Wha—" Jude starts when he notices the crapper erupting like Mount Vesuvius. "Stand back!" he yells like the goblin from Gringotts opening Vault 713.

"I'm trying!" I shout—but there's no where for me to go.

Too late, the toilet explodes.

Figuratively.

It *figuratively* explodes.

It's more like a geyser shoots forth and a fountain of water spews upward and outward.

"Ewwwww," I moan.

First vomit, now piss water?!

This is *not* my day!

Something pops out of the water and I scream, turning away from the snake mouth trying to eat me—except, when I turn, there's no snake. Just Jude. . .

And he's holding a fish—who turns into Theo.

"THEO!" I bellow in relief, hugging the naked wet man that Jude dropped when he shifted.

Everyone comes running to see.

"How—" I begin to ask.

"I'm a fish," Theo cuts me off.

Oh, yeah—duh.

That's one slippery dick, right there.

"I'm sorry I left yo—"

"Stop, mate," Theo cuts off Jude. "For once, I felt. . . *useful.*"

Jude gives a sharp nod.

"What happened?" he asks.

Theo leads me out of the bathroom and sits on a bed, pulling me next to him.

"There was a puddle near the backend of the car. I shifted and, when the jackal lunged for me, I sprung up into the silencer[1]."

"Theo!" Sian gasps. "You're lucky it wasn't still hot!"

"I know," he admits. "I'm very lucky—even luckier—the jackal shifter came at me again. I dropped from the muffler, but the git got his muzzle stuck in it! I had enough time to make it to the edge of the dock, shift, and follow the boat. Honestly, getting through the ship's pipes was more difficult than escaping the Secondary."

"Well, thank god! I was. . . devastated," I confess. "I thought you were dead."

Theo tugs me into his lap for a long hug.

It would be comforting—*if he weren't naked.*

It's hard to concentrate on anything but the feel of his dick against my ass. I squirm a bit, making him groan.

"Are there any clothes in those drawers?" Jude asks Arthur, who checks the dresser still blocking the door.

"Yes," Arthur answers, taking out some items. "Here, Theo, put these on. Belle, you can change into these."

I sigh.

It's better than sitting in a wet piss-water-vomit-stained tank and skirt, I suppose.

Giving Theo one last hug, I go back into the bathroom. There is a towel that I use to dry my hair and the floor before changing. The sleeves are long because it's clearly a man's shirt, but I easily roll the cuffs.

It's then that I notice something strange on my arm.

Pulling it closer, I nearly pass out—fur is poking out from underneath my skin.

I forgot about Dr. Fuckface and his experimental drug, but it all comes rushing back to me as I damn near turn into a freaking werewolf from my wrist to my elbow.

Son of a bitch.

This plot twist called my life just got even hairier.

THE END FOR NOW

CLICK HERE to get your copy of MYTH-BEHAVING (Shifters Anonymous Book 2)

Hold on to your titties—it's coming!

(And by titties, I obviously mean the bird. Sheesh. Like I'm some kind of slippery dick trying to sneak in dirty things.)

**CLICK HERE to get your copy of MYTH-BEHAVING
(Shifters Anonymous Book 2)**

ENDNOTES

CHAPTER SEVEN

1. An FYI for all my readers, I accidentally typed *penisively* at first, ahahaha. Clearly, Belle is not the only one with her head in the gutter.

CHAPTER NINE

1. British word for breasts
2. Another British word for breasts
3. British word to describe an idiot
4. British word for balls

CHAPTER TEN

1. British word for cops

CHAPTER TWELVE

1. Similar to the U.S. use of snarky—I like it. I plan on telling someone to stop being a narky-ass bitch someday. That's a lie. I probably won't. So, I'll have Belle use it somewhere in the story later. Carry on.
2. British word for 'tub/bathtub'
3. British idiom meaning 'to disparage one's own efforts/self'

CHAPTER FIFTEEN

1. British word for 'recon'
2. Similar to 'at the top of her lungs'
3. Brand of bug spray used in U.K.

CHAPTER EIGHTEEN

1. British word for attractive/hot
2. British word for whine
3. British word for underwear
4. British word for 'to finger'

CHAPTER TWENTY-ONE

1. British word for *insane*
2. British word for briefs/boxers
3. British word for sex/intercourse

CHAPTER TWENTY-FOUR

1. British word for stupid
2. British way of saying 'to get any'
3. British word for mutter/grumble

CHAPTER TWENTY-FIVE

1. British word for crazy/insane

CHAPTER THIRTY

1. British word for fit/tantrum

CHAPTER THIRTY-THREE

1. British word for paved road

CHAPTER THIRTY-SEX

1. British word for foul/disgusting
2. British word for junk
3. British word for booking it

CHAPTER THIRTY-EIGHT

1. British word for scientist

CHAPTER THIRTY-NINE

1. British word for boner

CHAPTER FORTY

1. British way of saying 'fired'

CHAPTER FORTY-ONE

1. British word for muffler

ACKNOWLEDGMENTS

Thank you to: Beth Ann for all promo work you've done with this book; Annie, Heather, and Allison for beta reading, Jodie-Leigh for the amazing cover and pro tip about 'fanny flutters', A.J. for formatting (and being sexy), all my ARCers, and to you, my reader.

ABOUT MJ MARSTENS

Bestselling author M.J. Marstens mixes romance, suspense, comedy, and sassy characters who can say whatever they are thinking because it is just a story. When she is not creating steamy scenes or laugh-out-loud fiascos, she is refereeing her three children that she homeschools. In her free time, she loves to eat, sleep, and pray that her children do not turn out like the characters she writes about in her books.

Stay Connected

Join the Reader's Group for exclusive content, teasers and sneaks, giveaways, and more:
https://www.facebook.com/groups/MJMarstensNR

ALSO BY MJ MARSTENS

Liminal Academy Series:

Book 1: Evanescent

Book 2: Ephemeral

Book 3: Eternal

The Afflicted Zodiac Series:

Book 1: Virgo Rising

Book 2: Retrograde

Book 3: Total Lunar Eclipse

Assassins of the Shadow Society Series:

Book 1: Badass Alchemy

Fairy Tales Retold for RH:

Adventures in Sugarland

Imprismed: Captured in Rainbowland

Classics Retold for RH:

The Swan Empress

Legends Retold for RH:

Scaled

Once Upon a Time in December

An Irrevent RH Comedy:

Motherf*cker

A Dark Menage:

Unveiled

An RH Paranormal Comedy:

Mate Date

Hexed, Vexed, & Undersexed co-write standalone with A.J. Macey:

Hexed, Vexed, & Undersexed

Glitter & Ghosts co-write series with A.J. Macey:

Books 1-4: Titles TBA